KINdred
Spirits

~

a novel

Nimmi Singh

◆ FriesenPress

Suite 300 - 990 Fort St
Victoria, BC, V8V 3K2
Canada

www.friesenpress.com

A note from the author:
Loving medieval history as I do, I thought it would be interesting to write
about a family living in such times. This story is about a fictional family, that
takes the reader through their lives' over a span of years.

ISBN
978-1-5255-0639-0 (Hardcover)
978-1-5255-0638-3 (Paperback)
978-1-5255-0637-6 (eBook)

1. FICTION, ALTERNATIVE HISTORY

Distributed to the trade by The Ingram Book Company

~

This book is dedicated to my dear son,
Shiv Singh

～

Foreword by the author:

Always a lover of anything medieval as I was growing up, I would lose myself in literature about that period, both fiction and non-fiction.

As a result, for years, I never had a good nights' sleep-with thoughts and images of fine lords and ladies floating about in my mind!

One day, as I was sitting at my computer desk, I decided to quickly type these jumbled thoughts, thus releasing them from my mind. A few months later, this book was born!

However, it never occurred to me to publish-these were, after all, private thoughts. But then I thought-well, why not?

In all this, I have even discovered a great love of writing. Book Two is well under way-there may be a sequel to this.

KINdred Spirits will not solve the world's problems-it was not created for that purpose. It will help the reader to run away from them, temporarily.

If the reader feels he/she has been able to temporarily go to another time, I will feel I have been successful in telling a story. Enjoy!

Nimmi Singh

Richard Carrington-Grey, Earl of Easterbrook
+Lady Elena Wyndham
    Anitra
      +Peter Gwynds,Duke of Pondshire
        Peter, Lord Pavis(1391)
          +Lady Isobel Treaves
            Mira(1412)
            Thomas(1412)
              +Moira Chadwick
                Serafina(1433)
                Miranda(1434)

        Louisa(1394)
          +Sir Marcus Mowbray
            Trenton(1414)
              +Arabella Ecks
                Arthur(1446)
                Cedric(1448)

    Ann-Marie
      +Sir Jon Ecks
        Edward(1400)
          +Lady Francesca Bains
            Nadia(1421)-married Peter Carrington-Grey

        Isabella(1400)
            Arabella(1416)-married Trenton Mowbray

    Maddelena
      +Sir Nicholas Prince

Richard Carrington-Grey, Earl of Easterbrook
+Lady Elena Wyndham
  Phillip
    +1. Lady Alice Pemberton
      Elena(1399)
        +Lord Michael Stafford
          Anthony, Lord Stafford(1416)
          Mary(1417)
          Alexander(1418)
          Richard(1419)
          Natalia(1420)
            +Theodore Albright
              Gwendolyn(1436)
              Matthew(1438)
              Letitia(1439)

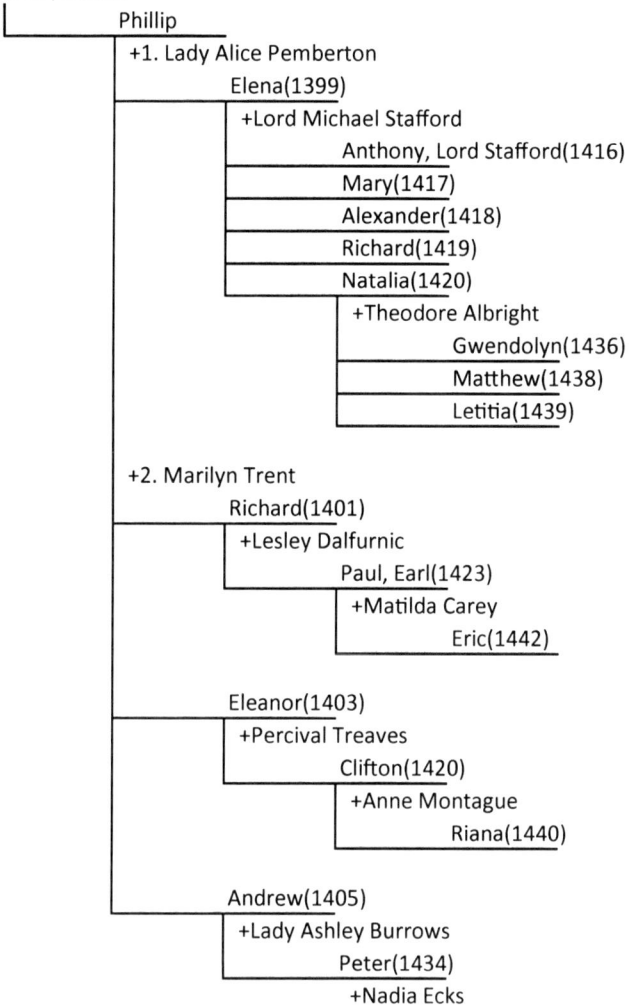

    +2. Marilyn Trent
      Richard(1401)
        +Lesley Dalfurnic
          Paul, Earl(1423)
            +Matilda Carey
              Eric(1442)

      Eleanor(1403)
        +Percival Treaves
          Clifton(1420)
            +Anne Montague
              Riana(1440)

      Andrew(1405)
        +Lady Ashley Burrows
          Peter(1434)
            +Nadia Ecks

Charles Carrington-Grey(1517)
+Lady Jaquelyn Devereux
    Edmund(1537)
    +Lady Elizabeth Calaigh
        Brandon(1557)
        +Deandra Bailey
            Anthony(1657)
            +Adriana Pomeroy
                Eva(1676)
                Cayden(1682)
                    Russel(1724)
                    +Margarita Clarke
                        Avery(1745)
                        Emma(1745)

Arthur(1526)-Charles' brother
+Samaira Chand
    Mina(1547)
    +Geoffrey Gaines, Duke of Ainsleigh
        Mason(1565)
        +Ellyn Pole
            Lucas(1637)
            +Charlotte Abbott
                Henry(1657)
                    Walter, Duke(1718)
                    +Madelyn Kensington
                      Peter(1738)

Descendants of the Stafford Line:
Mark, Lord Stafford(1638)
 +Maud Penhurst
         Sebastian(1668)
           +Lady Alicia Wallace
                 Simon(1690)
                   +Marlene McBride

         by Andrea Feeney
                 John Feeney(1695)
                   +Julia Haversleigh
                         Jordan, Earl(1714)
                           +Lady Camille Bancroft
                                 Roger(1733)

Descendants of Eleanor Carrington-Grey & Percival Treaves:
Phillip Treaves
 +Alys Duvall
         Belinda(1541)
         Jack(1545)
         James(1545)
           +Veronica Talbot
                 Aidan(1564)
                   +Lady Selena Wyndham
                 Nadia(1567)

         by Martine Ainsworth
                 Emma Ainsworth(1582)

Descendants of Trenton Mowbray & Arabella Ecks:
Thomas Mowbray(1628)
 +1. Lady Natalie Burrows

 +2. Anne Milligan
         Gabriel(1658)
           +Theresa Rice
         Daniel(1659)
         Sophia(1660)
           +Rev. Wilfrid Miller

～

1

Castle Colbert (1400)

L ADY Maddelena Carrington-Grey looked out of the window, her hair streaming down her back. As her eyes feasted on the beauty of the scenery outside Castle Colbert, she was unaware of the entry of another into the chamber. Lady Elena, Countess of Easterbrook, looked at her daughter with fondness, love, and pride, mingled with irritation.

Of the three daughters she had borne, this youngest of her's was the most stubborn, the most fearless, and the most beautiful. Every time she looked at this child of her's, she wondered how she could have given birth to such an exquisite being, when she herself was plain.

Her first born, Anitra, was a very beautiful young woman, with blond hair, and piercing blue eyes-she didn't stay in the single state for long-Lord Peter Gwynds, the Duke of Pondshire, swept her up in a very short space of time! Now, ten years later, she was very much a high-society lady, and a much sought-after hostess, living three months of the year with Peter in their beautiful London townhouse, going to and giving the most lavish parties. The other nine months of the year, they spent in Peter's country seat, with their two children, Peter and Louisa. All things considered, Anitra had done very well for herself, and Lady Elena felt she had done her duty right by her eldest.

Her second child, the only son and heir to the title, Philip, had a fair, clean-shaven face, auburn hair, and dark brown eyes-the image of his father, Lord Richard. Philip had an amazing sense of humour, and anyone near him, felt happy in his presence. Just four years ago, Peter married Lady Alice Pemberton, and there was a new baby in the nursery. Little Lady Elena, named after her grand-mother, filled the entire family with joy. At one year of age, she was spoiled by her grandparents, and aunts alike, as well as servants.

The third-born of the Carrington-Grey children, was Ann-Marie. With piercing blue eyes, framed by raven-black hair, Ann-Marie was another beauty. While visiting her older sister, Anitra, in London, she met Sir Jon Ecks at a ball, and the two fell in love immediately. They married two years ago, and were now expecting their first child. Lady Elena and her husband, the Earl, found they liked Jon very much. He was charming, kind, and utterly in love with their daughter.

And then, there was Maddelena, the youngest, and secretly, the Earl's favourite. With flaming auburn hair, and piercing green eyes, this child of her's was easily the most beautiful. Each of the other daughters could hold her own, as far as looks went, but Maddelena was exquisite. And the problem was, while the other girls cared about their looks, as girls should, Maddelena didn't. Lady Elena fretted about this. Philip came to her and said, one day, "Aw, Mums, don't fret. Maddy will soon see what a swan she really is."

"She already knows-she just doesn't care-and that's not right!

"She wears proper clothes and comports herself with the proper deportment, but in her attitude, she clearly doesn't care-and it shows! All she is interested in, are her books! That's not the proper attitude for an earl's daughter."

"Give her time," Philip counseled. "One day, she'll meet a man she'll fall head over heels with, and then she'll start to be glad she's beautiful."

Raising her hands up in frustration, the countess walked past her son. Maddelena had always been a favourite of his; he would defend her if she committed a crime. She smiled to herself as she thought-My children are truly amazing.

Later that evening, in their private chambers, the Earl was brushing his wife's hair as she looked in her mirror. It was a custom that had been going on since their wedding night, and both found it soothing, and comfortable. This was where both discussed private matters pertaining to each one's day. Living in a castle filled with servants and family, and retainers coming to and from the gates, there was no room for privacy. Just here, in the quiet of their rooms, there was privacy to be had.

"Richard," began the Countess. "I was thinking about the children today. Haven't you ever wondered how very different they are from us? Except for Philip, of course. He is your image. But look at the girls: Anitra, with her blond hair and blue eyes, and Ann-Marie-black-haired and blue- eyed, and Maddelena-auburn hair and green-eyed. They resemble neither you nor me. I have brown hair and brown eyes, and I was most unattractive when we married, but our children are so handsome."

The earl stared at his wife in the mirror. "My dear! What has brought on all this? And why do you call yourself unattractive? I married you because I love you."

"Richard, you are the sweetest of men. But you and I both know you married me because your parents set it up with mine-the dowry I brought with me was very great. It was a good bargain for both sides. But I do know, and I am so fortunate, that what started as a business contract turned into a marriage for love, for both of us. I love you too, dearest. Besides, I am a white-haired matriarch now, and my position has taught me one thing if nothing else: If you're a countess, your looks don't matter-people will bow to you regardless!

"No, I was just wondering-our daughters do not look like you or me. Ann-Marie, however, looks like your mother, the Lady Anne. So that's her. Anitra looks like my mother. But Maddy-I think she's a throwback to a few generations-maybe a great-great-or even another great-grandmother."

"Yes, and I know you've been worried about her. You shouldn't, you know. As you know, it's a Carrington-Grey tradition to educate ALL our children equally-daughters as well as sons. We wouldn't even consider Anitra and Ann-Marie marrying until they had completed their studies."

"Yes, love, and now, Maddelena has completed her's. But she doesn't want to marry. She wants to study more. She said she has soaked up her studies like a sponge, and she wants more! And before you tell me there's nothing wrong with that, I must tell you that the daughter of an earl MUST marry-she may study as much as she wishes, I have no objection. But marry, she must. She just wants to remain here at Castle Colbert, reading her books!"

The Earl smiled at his wife. "Alright, dear. We'll discuss this together with her soon. But tomorrow, Alice is bringing little Elena! I'm going to spend the day playing with that child. She doesn't come often-I miss her so."

"It's her mother. Alice keeps her away-on purpose, I'm sure. She knows how much we love her, and she keeps her away to get her revenge-for not accepting her in the beginning. Who could accept such a dour woman for a daughter-in-law?

"Do you remember when the marriage contracts were drawn up? You may not have seen it, you were conversing with her father. I was watching her: she was walking all around the room, weighing out the wealth of it in her mind. And not one smile did she give my Philip-or anyone, for that matter. And she's such a snob-she can't wait for Philip to be Earl, so she can be Countess. And she treats the servants like they are nobodies. Someone should tell her it's the Carrington-Grey habit to treat all people with equality and kindness, be they servant or master. She's the Countess of Snobbery and No Manners, if you ask me!"

"Yes, dear, I agree, she isn't the most agreeable person in the world, but would she keep her child away from us? Philip wouldn't allow that."

"Philip has always been a lover of peace-he and Alice are so ill-suited. He will have peace at any price, even his own happiness, while she will disrupt it--at any time. Well, I, too, am looking forward to my granddaughter's visit. And I'll be civil to my daughter-in-law."

"You always are, my dear! Trust you to never let your true feelings show-you may not have been born a countess, but one would never know-it's been bred into your very bones!" And, laughing, the Earl and Countess of Easterbrook retired for the night.

2

Castle Colbert (1400)

THE next morning, Lord Richard and Lady Elena were break-ing their fast, when Philip walked in with a springy step. An outsider could be forgiven for thinking this young man was a simple commoner-except for his resemblance to his father. He was dressed, as usual, very simply. Like his sister, Maddelena, Philip understood the need for pomp and ceremony, but he believed it had its place.

"So sorry I'm late for breakfast," the young man bent to kiss his mother on the cheek. "I decided to sleep in this morning. I thought I'd have a good rest before Lady Alice makes her grand entrance."

"Philip! You speak of your wife! Try to show a little more respect."

"Mother, you don't even like her. I must live with her, because she's my wife, but I love to come here, too-the atmosphere and love here is so much kinder. Since Elena was born, I thought it would be better, but it hasn't. And since Alice refuses to come, except when she feels she must, then I have no choice but to leave Bently Manor once in awhile to clear my head."

"Maybe she would be more loving if you didn't leave her so often," suggested the Earl.

"Trust me, Father, we've done that. I think it's gotten to the point where's she's almost relieved when I come on these little visits. But even if she's not, who cares? Lack of love in a marriage can lead to friendship, or starting to care, but complete indifference drives a man to just not caring anymore. All my earlier attempts to build on our marriage met with failure. So now, to keep peace-in my home and in my head, I go my way, and she goes her's."

"Oh, my poor dear boy! But what of little Elena? Where is she in all this?" said the countess.

"She is well cared for. One thing I'll say, Alice is a good mother, except she keeps her from you. But in all else, she is good-and I love the child to distraction. And Miss Trent, her nanny, is also crazy about the child, and the child adores her. So, neither of you need to worry about her. Now, after this rousing speech, I'm starving!" Lord Bently grabbed some food off the sideboard, and sat down.

As the three occupants of the dining room ate, Maddelena walked into the room. She was wearing a simple turquoise gown, with a contrasting red belt hanging down from her slim waist. Her beautiful hair was pulled back into a long, thick braid, dropping down to her waist.

Muttering a "Good morning" to the others, she helped herself to breakfast.

Lady Elena decided to forego the little chat she had planned to have with her. Now was not the time, or place. She was going to do that chat privately, in her office.

"Sit down, my dear. Good news! Elena is coming for a few days! Isn't that lovely?"

"Elly? Oh, I can't wait! Will Alice be coming, too? Oh, sorry, Philip."

"No need to apologize, Maddie. I know you need to get your armour at the ready."

"Stop it, both of you," said their mother, as a page boy walked in.

"A message for Lady Elena!" The young boy handed the missive to the countess, and left the room.

"Oh my!" The countess had tears in her eyes! Her husband looked at her, "What is it, love?"

"This is from Ann-Marie. She writes that she and Jon had twins last month!!! A boy and a girl they have named Edward and Isabella. Ann-Marie also says both she and the babies are all recovered and would like to come for a visit next week. Oh, by all that's wonderful! I must also write to Anitra. I would like her to come, too. It's been so long since she has visited, and every time a new family member has been born, we all get together. It's a good thing Alice is coming. I will persuade her to lengthen her visit." The countess rose from the table and hurried off to her private office.

The earl looked at his wife's departure with a little grin. "It appears we are grandparents-yet again!" He could not hide the proud gleam in his eyes.

"And we're Aunts-and Uncle-again!" said Maddelena. "Oh, I can't wait to see the babies-and Elly, too! And Ann-Marie and Jon, too, of course!" No one made notice, or replied, that she did not mention her sister-in-law.

3

Castle Colbert (1400)

"LADY Bently," announced the butler. Alice Carrington-Grey, Lady Bently, née Pemberton, glided into the drawing room of the large castle. She had on a dove-grey gown, and her dark hair was pulled back in a chignon. She smiled at the Earl and Countess, but her eyes remained cold.

"My lord Earl, my lady Countess, I give your good greeting," she very slightly lowered her head in the form of a bow.

"Maddelena, how good it is to see you again," but her tone spoke just the opposite. "My lord husband, Philip, how are you?"

"Very well, Alice. And you?" Philip's speech was stilted. Anyone would think that these two people were strangers. Lady Alice looked towards the door she had come through and said, "Bring her in!" A slim, attractive young woman brought in a little girl of a year's age. Elena Carrington-Grey was the image of her father and grandfather, with auburn hair and brown eyes. "Poppy!" The child screamed with joy, and lunged herself onto her father. Philip laughed, his feelings forgotten, and threw the girl in the air and caught her. Elly screamed to do it again.

"Stop it! There's no doing with her when you do that!" replied Alice.

Philip put his daughter down-" Go see Grandpa and Grandam-they've been waiting for you!"

Elena ran to her grandparents and received her share of hugs and kisses. Then she got another share from Aunt Maddy.

Philip walked over to the slim young woman. He turned to his family. "This is Miss Marilyn Trent, Elena's nanny. She is remarkable with her, and Elly loves her." Then, knowing how it would irritate his wife, and not able to resist, he turned to Miss Trent, and said, "Thank you, Miss Trent. You're doing a wonderful job."

Hearing Alice's sharp intake of breath at the same time he saw the nanny blush, and reply, "Oh, you're very welcome, my lord. And it's no trouble at all. I love Lady Elena like my own." This last was a mistake. Alice turned to the nanny and said, "That will do, Miss Trent. You may leave now. You will be summoned when she needs washing up for dinner." The nanny curtsied and left the room.

"A bit uncalled for, don't you think?" Philip had to say this to this person, with whom he shared his bed for four years, with whom he had a child. But each time they met, in their married, living-together-but-sometimes-apart life, he felt he knew her less and less; and what he did know, he found he disliked more and more. His marriage was a contracted one, like his parents', but unlike his parents' marriage, which had blossomed into love, his had blossomed into hate. The dowry was good, everything was good-on paper, it was the perfect marriage, but, in reality, it was a disaster.

Alice turned to look at him. "Why? Do you desire her?"

Maddy sucked in her breath. The Earl cleared his throat and looked away. Only the countess looked directly at her daughter-in-law. She got up from her place on the chair. Walking directly to Alice, she said, in a low voice, "You and your husband will not speak like this in front of your child. And you, Alice, will not speak such things. If you wish to discuss it, do it away from my granddaughter. And away from the rest of us, too, I might add. We do not wish to know of your marital issues. Do I make myself clear? And furthermore, one thing I will say before we close this subject: If the two of you even cared the slight bit for each other, the possibility of such a thing happening would never arise. From the beginning, you never showed even a small amount of love for my son. And I know he was prepared to love you. Well, it is over, now. But you are Lady Bently, one day soon to be the Countess, so conduct yourself as befits a member of this family. Once again, do I make myself clear?"

Alice backed a step away. She had never seen her mother-in-law like this. While she had sensed from the beginning that the Countess didn't care for her, she had always shown her civility. That was probably over, and it was her's, Alice's, fault.

Lady Elena walked back to her chair, picking up her grand-daughter on the way. "By the way, Alice, I'm going to ask you to lengthen your stay. Ann-Marie has had twins, and she and her family are coming in a few days. I've written to Anitra, and she and her family are also coming. So, we are ALL going to be together as a family to welcome the newest additions. And, Alice, that was not a request-you will stay." The Earl and Countess, with their grand-daughter, left the room.

"I'm leaving. I have to go look through some of my books." Maddelena beat a hasty retreat. She could sense something brewing between husband and wife, and she didn't want to remain on the scene, although a secret part of her wished her brother would start an association with the pretty, pleasant nanny.

"It appears we have been given some privacy." Philip sprawled on a chair. "I don't know why-you and I really have nothing more to say to each other. And my mother is right-don't talk like that in front of them, and especially not in front of Elly. And you know very well there's nothing between me and Miss Trent, although the way things are going between you and me..." And so saying, he, too, got up and left the room.

Lady Alice Bently stood in the middle of an empty drawing room. She hated coming here. She loved the castle, but she hated dealing with her in-laws, especially her autocratic mother-in-law. The Earl was easier to talk to, but Alice sensed he also disapproved of her. Maddalena was Philip's pet-she stuck up for him, he stuck up for her. If Philip didn't care for something, neither did she. As a result, her relationship with her youngest sister-in-law was not a pleasant one. Anitra had been married too long, and was too involved with her husband and family to really care either way. Ann-Marie was always quiet-one never knew what she was thinking.

Her husband's implications about seeing someone didn't bother her-she only married him to eventually win her way to becoming a countess-and he, she, and the whole family, were aware of the fact.

4

Castle Colbert (1400)

Six days later, the family was seated at the dinner table. Surrounding the Earl and Countess, was Maddelena, Philip, Alice, Anitra and her husband, Peter, and Ann-Marie, and her husband, Jon. It was a loud, happy group. The children had eaten their dinners, and visited their elders. There was Peter and Louisa, Anitra's children. Peter, at nine, and his sister, at six, were very excited about the new additions. Peter, as the oldest grandchild, felt he should reign supreme in the Carrington-Grey nursery, but he was kept in check. Next, was pretty little Louisa, looking just like her mother. After that, was Elena, Philip's and Alice's daughter. Although only a year old, she trailed after her older cousin, Louisa, and copied her in everything she did. Then, of course, the babies. Edward, and Isabella-both safe and snug in the nursery. All the children had eaten, and now slept, while the adults feasted.

Lady Elena looked around the table-this is what she loved the most: all of her children here together. She hadn't seen her eldest, Anitra, for two years. It was so good to see her again.

Alice stood up. "If you will all excuse me. I have a headache, and will retire. Good night."

After she left, Anitra whispered, "What's happening with her? We've been here two days, and the whole time, she's looked as if she's sucked on a lemon."

Maddelena giggled, while Philip laughed. "Sister dear," he replied. "You haven't seen her for so long, you've forgotten that is her regular expression."

Ann-Marie shook her head. "Phil. It's just too bad. I've spoken to her. Why won't she change? People can change, you know."

"Maybe some people do. But she never will. The first three years, I tried. Now I don't bother."

Ann-Marie looked down at her plate. "She told me she married you for the title, to eventually become a countess, and that you and she both know it."

"Yes, I know it. But how could she tell you? I know you all are aware of it, but to blatantly say it out like that. My god, will she never end this? I have a good mind to seek an annulment. Then she will never get what she wants."

"Philip, you can't! You're married to her!"

"And does that mean I have to become so unhappy? There is no happiness for me-her's is only the title, for me, nothing."

"She'll fight you," this, quietly, from Maddelena. "She'll fight you because she'll want the title, no matter how unhappy she may be in the actual marriage. And if she can't get the title, she'll hold

Elly as hostage."

"No!" The Earl banged his fist on the table. "I like to think I'm a fair man. I've always liked to look at things from both sides, but over the past few days, I've seen enough. Son, if you favour an annulment, we'll discuss it and I'll have it drawn up with my lawyers. And Elly will not suffer-we're a powerful family, and what good is power if not to protect our own? Also, I'll talk to Alice. We will all try to do the best thing-for the child, and for the both of you, too. It isn't healthy for either of you-being in a relationship like this. I'll return her dowry to her, and she will be free to pursue a marriage, if she wants. I will also have my lawyers draw up stipulations about Elena. She is a Carrington-Grey--the granddaughter of the Earl, and she cannot be held as a bargaining tool."

"Thank you, husband," smiled the Countess. "An annulment is such a drastic procedure, but our's, or, rather, Philip's, has become a drastic situation. We will leave all this to you, dearest, since you are the diplomat of diplomats!"

5

Castle Colbert (1415)

LORD Philip Carrington-Grey, Earl of Easterbrook, sat in one of the cozy chairs in the library, reading his book, as he looked up, and smiled at the occupant of the other cozy chair. Sensing his smile, Lady Marilyn, Countess of Easterbrook, smiled back. Fifteen years had passed, and Philip's contentment knew no bounds. Since that meeting with his family, and his father's promise to do something, something had definitely been done. The Earl of Easterbrook was a powerful man, and with his influence, the annulment went under way, and quite amazingly easily.

The family had been right: Alice put up a fight-she was a snob-and her current title as Baroness Bently, and future one as Countess, meant everything to her. But in that private meeting with the old Earl, the Earl explained to her in no uncertain terms, that even if she chose not to divorce his son, he would see to it that she would never inherit the title. Furthermore, because of her stubbornness, he would arrange to strip her of the title of Baroness Bently. Both titles would be hereditarily passed on to her daughter-should she wish to stay married to Philip, she would be known simply as Mistress Carrington-Grey. However, the Earl said he was prepared to be generous. He would return to Alice all of her dowry, with a little extra, if she agreed to the annulment. When Alice realized that fighting over a title she would never get was futile, then a lot of money eased her pain.

What angered her beyond telling was her ex-husband's next move. Three months after the dissolution of his marriage, Philip started courting Marilyn Trent, his daughter's nanny. Soon, they became man and wife. Shortly, after the old Earl died, Alice's greatest rival became the Countess, donning the cloak of the one title Alice herself had coveted for years. The difference was, Marilyn cared nothing for the title-she just loved the man who gave it to her. The marriage caused a minor scandal, at first, but after the Dowager Countess saw how happy her son now was, she could only give her warmest blessings.

As for Maddelena, she finally met the man of her dreams-Sir Nicholas Prince. They married and two years ago, they had a little baby girl-Alexandra, who was the image of her mother. Maddelena knew she finally warmed her mother's heart by marrying, and she was only glad that she could do it in her own time and terms. She kept up with her studies-she felt she was still 'a sponge soaking up knowledge.'

Most of the grandchildren were grown up. Her eldest, Peter, married Lady Isobel Treaves, and they now had three children-Mira, Mina, and Thomas. Peter's sister, Louisa, married Sir Marcus Mowbray, and their son, Trenton, was a delight. And then there was her namesake, Elena, who could do no wrong in her eyes, and Philip's three children with Marilyn: Richard, Eleanor, and Andrew. And the twins of the family-Edward and Isabella, now fifteen years old-each thinking with and for one another. Finally, Maddelena's daughter, Alexandra, a beautiful fairy-like child. The Dowager countess smiled-her Richard would be so proud. Looking back at all the years and things the family had been through, her troubles regarding Maddy's married state, or lack of it, seemed so inconsequential. All the children's and grandchildren's spouses were wonderful, and everything seemed good. Everything had a way of working out. Except Richard's absence-oh, how she missed him.

Elena, was now sixteen years old, and as sweet and pretty as a young girl could be. She loved her step-mother, who was once her nanny. Besides her, Philip had three more children: fourteen-year-old Richard, now Lord Bently on the death of the old Earl, and his father's ascendancy to the title, twelve year-old Eleanor, and ten year-old Andrew.

The whole family was much saddened by the death of the old Earl, especially the Countess. But his presence lived on in the old castle. As for the Dowager Countess, Elena, she lived in a manor house of her own. Being asked by her son and new daughter-in-law to live with them, she refused. She felt better in her own manor. She had raised her family in Colbert Castle, and it was now Philip's turn to raise his.

And Alice? Philip's first wife never re-married. She purchased a manor house as far from the Carrington-Greys as she could find, and went travelling to the Continent as often as she could. Although given the opportunity to have her daughter live with her, partially, she refused. She saw Elena's fondness for her step-mother, and personally would have preferred it if the girl hated her. Therefore, she felt, Elena was better off with her father. And she was better off not hearing about the many attributes of Marilyn.

What did Elena think? At sixteen, she already knew the situation, and her mother's vague excuses did not fool her. She knew she wasn't wanted. She sometimes felt bothered that it didn't bother her so much. You would think that any person being rejected by their mother would feel bad. But she didn't. She felt so much love from her father, her step-mother, half-brothers, and half-sister, that she didn't feel anything lacking.

This is the situation Philip wanted to discuss with his wife. He had been thinking about his firstborn. And he was concerned. He was aware when Alice sent back the note about her refusal to have her own daughter over. Philip couldn't believe it: her own daughter!

"My love," he looked at Marilyn. Then, abandoning the cozy chair for the love seat, he gave a tap beside him, indicating he wished his wife near. As she obliged, he continued, "As you know, I'm concerned about that witch's note-her rejection of Elena is beyond imagination! My mother would have palpitations if she knew!"

The countess held a finger to his lips. "Firstly, dear, you must not call her 'witch.' Yes, I don't like her, either, in fact, I can't stand her, and what she's doing to Elena is abominable, but she is her mother-the mother of your first child. My main concern is not her, but how this affects Elena; she is all that should matter."

"You're right-and Elena is all that matters in this situation. But you must admit; she has a nerve."

"Now," replied Marilyn. "The reason for her rejection is plain: Elena is from her life with you-she is a Carrington-Grey, and Alice wants no more of that. Furthermore, Elena loves me, and Alice can't bear it. However, you can put your mind at ease. I overheard her saying to Maddy that she was so happy here, with all the love, that she didn't feel rejected by Alice at all. And that was what was bothering her-that she felt nothing for her mother."

"Really? Well, as you know, Alice was always cold. I gave her credit for at least being a good mother, if nothing else, but I think I'll have to retract that. I don't think she showed that child an ounce of love."

Marilyn replied, "I don't mean to say anything against her-I promised myself when we married that I wouldn't. But, no, she didn't. All the general looking-after of the child was delegated to myself and other staff. She may have put an arm around her at times, but to actually hug, cuddle, and play with her, then I can definitely say, no, she did not."

"Well, if what you say is true, then I'm not going to bring it up with Elena. I don't want to disturb her. And I'm certainly not going to tell Mother. She'll end up by marching down to Alice and hauling her over the coals-then refuse to let her see her anyway. Actually, Mother is probably the best one to deal with her!"

"Don't you dare! Let's let sleeping dogs lie. Now, is there any family happening this weekend? Should I be prepared for an onslaught, or just a minor invasion?"

Philip smiled. How very different was this second wife of his! And thank God for it!

"As a matter of fact, I received a note from Peter yesterday."

"Peter, Lord Pavis, or Peter the Duke?" Marilyn bantered, naming the son and the father.

"The Duke-and Anitra, of course. Apparently, Peter said Anitra wants to come to Colbert for a quick visit, and could we send for Mother, too, as she would like a visit with her."

"Alright, I'll pen a note to the Dowager Countess. I'm sure she will come." And with that, Lady Marilyn left the room to write her note.

6

Castle Pondshire (1415)

L ADY Anitra Gwynds, the Duchess of Pondshire, sat in a very strange-looking chair in the drawing-room of her castle. It was large, and was stuffed with feathers, making it very soft and comfortable. It had been made especially for her by a furniture maker in the village of Pondshire. Her legs were propped up on a footstool.

Fifteen years had not been kind to her. It would be hard to recognize in this woman the same beautiful eldest daughter of the Earl of Easterbrook. Over the years, she had run to fat. If she walked too far or too fast, she puffed or panted, and her legs always gave her great pain. Her face, too, had gotten fat, but if one looked, one could still see those famous, piercing blue eyes, framed by the still famously-beautiful blonde hair.

The castle loomed large and empty, since Peter and Louisa had married and moved away. However, they frequently visited their parents, and when they did, the sound of their children's voices filled the ancient castle's corridors, much to everyone's delight.

The Duchess was working on a tapestry when her husband walked into the room.

"Dearest love. I've received a reply from Marilyn. She wrote that she's sent a note to Mother, and hopefully she'll come, too."

"Wonderful! It'll be nice to go to Colbert again. My goodness, did you notice Philip last time we were there? I didn't know he could be so happy! I'm so pleased for him at last-Marilyn is a very good wife to him-and a wonderful step-mother to Elena."

"She's a better step-mother to Elly than Alice is a mother to her," muttered Peter.

"Alright, husband, but Alice is a path we simply do not want to go to anymore. Let's be sunny. There has been enough darkness in poor Philip's and Elly's lives-so let's not add to it by mentioning the cause."

"Alright, my Lady Duchess, your wish is my command," and so saying, Peter bent down and tenderly kissed his wife. "How are your legs feeling today, my dear?"

"Much better today, thank you. Our things are ready to leave in the morning. Now, dear, it's time for dinner, then we shall have an early night, as we must make an early start in the morning."

And so saying, the Duke and Duchess of Pondshire walked hand in hand to the dinner table.

7

Colbert Castle (1415)

I T was a comfortable group. Dinner was over, and had been cleared up by the servants. The family was seated in the small private drawing room. Apart from the Earl and Countess, there was the Duke and Duchess, and the Dowager Countess. The children had their meal with the adults earlier-a custom which the Dowager Duchess did not approve of-and now they had retired.

"How are you feeling, dear?" This from Lady Elena.

"I'm fine, Mother. I may not look as I once did, but I feel quite well. Apart from my legs, of course. But for the past few days, they've been alright, too."

Philip looked at his family. He decided to come out with what he had been thinking. He hadn't even mentioned it to his wife.

"Peter, Anitra, I know it was your idea to come, but within a few days, or weeks, I would have invited you over anyway. Along with Mother. I have had something in mind, and it's concerning my Elly. And I think Mother, and you, Anitra, are best suited to help me tackle this."

Philip certainly could not complain he didn't get anyone's attention with his little speech!

Lady Elena already had an idea what her son was referring to. "Are you, by chance, asking about arranging a possible marriage for her, Philip?"

Philip heaved a sigh of relief. "Yes, Mother, I am." Turning to his wife, he said, "Sorry I haven't mentioned this to you, dear, but I've been so worried about this, I didn't want to worry you."

Marilyn replied, "It's alright, dear. Now let's hear the opinions of the experts!" And she smiled at her mother-in-law and sister-in-law. Lady Elena smiled back-she really liked this woman!

"Philip, firstly, shouldn't this be something you consult Alice with? Forgive me, Marilyn, but, although I know your marriage with her is over, the fact remains, Alice is still Elly's mother," said Peter.

"Thanks for that, Peter. But to be perfectly blunt, Alice has rejected Elly completely. It seems Elly was talking too favourably about Marilyn, so Alice just refused to keep her with her anymore. As a result, she has given up the privilege of being called 'mother.'"

"Alice has WHAT?" The Dowager Countess got up from her chair.

"Easy, Mother, I didn't want to tell you, and for this reason. But not to fear: Elly is perfectly happy here, and misses Alice not at all. Now, back to the topic at hand."

"Well, to be honest, I have been out of the social scene for far too many years. Anitra is the best one for this. I do know of some of the old families, though. However, the personality of the person-that is something Anitra would know." The Dowager Countess looked at her daughter.

The Duchess, in turn, looked at her brother. She had been thinking possible candidates the minute he mentioned his mission.

"Well, I have a few names in mind, Philip. My personal best choice, is Michael Stafford. He is the only son of the Earl Stafford. And I've met him-he's handsome, charming, but most important, he's simply a very nice young man."

"The Staffords are a very old, grand family-not as grand as the Carrington-Greys, of course, but still quite grand," remarked the Dowager Countess.

"Now Mums," replied Philip, using his old pet name for her. "According to you, no family is as grand as the Carrington-Greys!"

"Stop that, dear boy!"

After the banter had subsided, Anitra patiently continued. "There is also Sir Francis Trilby, but he's a little old for her, I think. Oh, I should have mentioned. Michael Stafford is twenty, Sir Francis is thirty-two."

"What about his family, and what's he like?" asked Lady Elena.

"Sir Francis is knight errant, and his father was a knight. The family is not a great name." replied Anitra.

"Then we cannot consider him," replied her mother. "Age is not the issue-girls marry old men-a man of thirty-two to a girl of sixteen is nothing. However, one thing we DO have to consider, is the fact that Sir Francis does not come from a noble house."

Philip leaned forward. "Mother, you didn't come from a noble house-and Marilyn certainly didn't, either. It seems alright-I don't see the difference."

Lady Elena looked at her son, and there was a hint of amusement in her eyes as she replied to his statement.

"You don't see the difference, Philip? Well, then I shall instruct you. A commoner may marry a noble, provided she is not a peasant. Neither dear Marilyn, nor I, fit the mould of peasant. My father was a rich knight, and Marilyn's father was a gentleman. Now, women, when they marry, take on their husband's name and title. That being said, do you want your daughter to go from the title of an earl's daughter to just plain Mistress So-and-So? So, that is why. She must marry someone of equal or higher birth."

Philip looked down, quietly held his wife's hand. He was trying so hard not to laugh, and he knew that his wife, and his mother, were, too.

Anitra looked around. "May we continue? So, as I said, Michael Stafford-son of an earl. And Francis Trilby, son of a knight. There is also Lord Geoffrey Beltine, I believe he is an Earl, but I don't know too much about him."

"Well, I don't want to consider him," said Philip. "Not knowing about him, I don't want to thrust Elly into an awful situation." Memories of his first marriage came flooding back, and he snuggled up to his wife.

"It seems young Stafford might be best. First, we'll inform Elly," said the Dowager Countess.

8

Castle Colbert (1415)

"B ut I don't want to marry-ever," Elena announced to her family when she was told.

"Nonsense. The daughter of an earl marries-she must, and you, my dear young lady, will do as she is told." Elena looked at her formidable grandmother.

"No! Not me!" And she was about to run, when Marilyn held her hand.

"My dear, I know what this is about. You are thinking about your father's marriage with your mother, and what a disaster it was. But look at me-we are so happy together. And your grandparents were so happy together, and Uncle Peter and Aunt Anitra, too." She wanted her step-daughter to be eased into this gently. After all, the marriage of the eldest daughter of the Earl of Easterbrook was something that would definitely happen-but Marilyn felt Elly should accept it-gradually-just not too gradually.

9

Stafford Castle (1435)

SITTING in her drawing room, thirty-six-year-old Lady Elena, Dowager Countess of Stafford, was sitting, sewing, while she was contemplating her family. That is, her family, such as it was. All of the older generation, including her father, step-mother, mother, aunts, and uncles, were all dead. Dead, too, was her formidable, but beloved grandmother, the Dowager Countess of Easterbrook. Elena found she missed them all-even her cold mother. With the absence of the older generation, she felt like a full adult, truly alone.

Elena smiled to herself as she thought that. How could one truly be alone in a castle filled with children, and servants? But, one could, inside.

She looked back at the day when she was told she would have to marry. Very shortly after that-six weeks after, in fact, she was married, to Michael Stafford, the only heir to the Earldom.

Michael had not been a bad sort, really. While their marriage had never fostered any feelings of great love, or passion, it had been one of mutual friendship, liking, and respect. Elena felt that was better than nothing, then realized she was much better off then a lot of people.

It was fifteen years ago, while she was pregnant with her fifth child, that Michael met with a fatal accident; his horse through him, and he landed on the frosty earth, head first. He died immediately, and their oldest son, Anthony, became the next Earl of Stafford, at the very tender age of four.

Elena smiled when she thought of her first-born. He was secretly her favourite. Now, at nineteen years of age, the handsome young earl had burnished auburn hair, and blue eyes. She was sure he set young hearts a-flutter! A bride would have to be found for him, and soon. She would think this over. She knew her half-sister, Eleanor, married a distant relation of cousin Thomas' mother. The Treaves family was very highly thought-of. She'll see what she could do. She didn't anticipate trouble from Tony-he did anything she asked!

Her second child, Mary, was eighteen, and a very different kettle of fish indeed. For poor Mary had taken after her great grand-mother in looks-she was very plain. While the old Countess had strength of will and character, Mary was quiet as a mouse, and never wanted to speak, unless someone spoke to her. She was a studious young woman, like her great aunt Maddelena. Elena knew that with her wealth and title, she would be easy to marry off, but she didn't really know this daughter of her's-what made her tick, her likes, dislikes. She wanted to provide happy mar-riages, if possible, for all her children. In this world, marriages were nothing but contracts, but they demanded intimacy between the two people in the contract-so some thought had to be taken. Elena felt the generations before her had not really taken this into account-hence, her father's disastrous first marriage to her mother. Elena knew the inevitability of marriage-in her world of nobility, people simply did not remain single-except...she put that thought inside her head for another time.

After Mary, came seventeen-year-old Alexander. He was the imp of the family. Always playing practical jokes on everyone, and taking nothing seriously. His mother prayed for the day when he would grow out of this.

Richard came next. Only sixteen years of age, this child of her's was as serious as Alex was impish. He was always to be found, in a corner of the castle, reading a book.

Her last child, the child her husband never saw, was Natalia. Now fifteen, she felt that of all her children, Natalia was the most trouble. For her daughter had, at a very early age, discovered her liking for the opposite sex. Well, Elena realized she would have to marry her off much earlier than was normal-or there would be very unpleasant consequences. She was going to look for a husband for her even before she looked for a wife for Anthony. She could sense the import of this.

Going to her writing desk, the Dowager Countess sat down to write.

10

Stafford Castle (1435)

"Ma, you're not going to have me get married the same time as Nattie, are you? It's-it's shaming!" So saying, the young Earl belied his feelings by laughing. He knew the reasons for his mother's rush.

"No, she will wed before you. Girls can wed before their older brothers-it's no shame. But, it is something I'm determined on. Nothing she, you, or anyone, says will dissuade me in this. And I am giving her very little choice as to whom I select."

"But you've always been telling us, that because of your childhood experiences with your parents, you want better ones for us."

Elena looked at her son. "That's true, but in this case, I believe speed is of the essence. I don't know what's gotten into your sister, no amount of discipline is helping. No, it shall be done, and immediately."

11

Henley House (1445)

LADY Natalia Albright, née Stafford, looked out of her bedroom window, at the bright sun streaming through the panes. The world outside was beautiful. The world inside was beautiful, too-the Albright seat of Henley House was a lovely, though modest manor house. Natalia loved it.

However, that is as far as her happy feelings went. She had never forgiven her mother. She was forced into this marriage, and it was a most unsuitable one. She didn't like her husband-and she knew Teddy didn't much care for her. He was away most of the time, and she was sure he saw other women-and this didn't bother her-more proof of her indifference, and his. At the time of her wedding, she learned that Teddy was also being forced-as the oldest, his marriage was paramount, and Natalia was a good catch, although she was quite young for a bride-only fifteen. At first, both bride and groom felt sympathy-both of their plights were the same-but they were so ill-matched, the sympathy couldn't last. Over the years, they got more and more distant with each other. Teddy was never unkind to her-but theirs's was not a house of warmth.

Her children, Gwendolyn, Matthew, and Letitia, were nine years and under, still at the wonderful age to love. However, Natalia found she could not love them. Because she was forced into a marriage with their father, she just could not. Most mothers in this situation would derive comfort in their children, but she could not-they were Teddy's children, too, and she could not give them that love-and, unfortunately, they were all too aware of it. Teddy adored them, but she was not the maternal kind. This was another bone of contention between her and her own mother. Elena felt her daughter should not be treating her children so coldly. Natalia pointed out that their father gave them enough love for the both of them.

12

Castle Colbert (1445)

Seven-year-old Matthew Albright raced out of the school-room at breakneck speed, bumping into a maidservant carry-ing a fresh load of laundry, which spilled all over the floor, like a small mountain of white.

"Maister Matthew! Have a care!" And she reached down to get the washing, which would have to be re-done. But it was hard to be annoyed with this child. He had such a sunny disposition, and saw good wherever he went.

"I'm so sorry!" And Matthew bent down to help the maid.

He turned the corner, walking at a more moderate pace. He loved this castle-home of his family on his mother's side. He wasn't a Carrington-Grey, of course-he was an Albright. And his mother was a Stafford. But his grandmother Elena was a Carrington-Grey. So that had to count for something. Colbert was the seat from which all Carrington-Greys sprung.

He and his sister, Gwen, had been sent here for their studies. Their cousin, Paul, was the current Earl, with his wife, Matilda as Countess. Matthew loved his older cousin and his wife. They had an adorable three-year-old son named Eric, who was fussed and petted by the whole household. Matilda was a very sweet woman who encouraged much play, as well as study. She said balance was important. As for cousin Paul, all he wanted to do was play! Although twenty-two years old, and full of responsibility as an earl as well as a husband and father, Paul Carrington-Grey was a very happy-go-lucky type of person. He also understood the importance of family, and that there wasn't much enjoyment at the home of his cousin, Natalia, so he encouraged the two older children to come and study here. Natalia's youngest, Letitia, was only six years old, and her father would not part with her. So the little girl remained at home.

13

Castle Colbert (1445)

T HE next evening, the family was having a quiet time in the drawing room. The meal had been consumed and cleared. Now, as the digestive process occurred, people began to relax, and sift through the events of the day. Paul was having a game of chess with the castle chaplain, while Matilda was sewing on a tapestry. She was at a particularly delicate place in it, and she was frowning in concentration. Baby Eric had, of course, been put to bed, but Matthew and Gwendolyn were still up. Matthew sensed their bedtime was going to be announced very soon.

As he got himself prepared for it, the steward walked into the room, and addressing Paul, he said, "My lord, a young lady has just come, she says she is your cousin." There was a slight inflection in his tone, indicating he was questioning the veracity of the statement.

That very inflection told Paul this was unusual.

"Bring the lady in here." Paul noticed the butler referred to her as 'lady' and not 'woman'. His butler's snob button never failed him! So, the lady was well-bred. But who could she be? He knew all his cousins-at least he thought he did.

A young lady walked into the room. She had long black hair, and piercing blue eyes. "My lord, you do not know me, but I am your cousin. My name is Arabella. Let me tell you just how we are related.

"Firstly, I know that the last earl, your father, was named Richard. His father before him was Philip-son of the first Earl. Now, me: my mother's name was Isabella. And her mother was Ann-Marie, who was the sister of Philip. There! Now do you understand?"

"Yes, of course!" Paul clapped his hands. "I should like to draw up a tree of our family-it would be interesting. But, tell me, of all our family, you, I have never seen. Why is that?"

Arabella sat in one of the chairs. "It's very simple, really. Shame, I suppose. You see, my mother, Isabella, did not marry my father. She had a tendresse for a man she could not marry because he was already betrothed to another. Her father was a very loving man, but he couldn't allow her to marry an unavailable man, so my mother took the matter into her own hands. She ran off with him. I was born nine months later. The man eventually married his betrothed. My mother kept away from the family she knew would shun her. Well, she is dead now-everyone is dead. I had to come-I felt a great need to meet you-I've never had family-and I ache to know every single one of you."

"Well, then, of course you shall." Matilda came over to sit with Arabella. "We could have a family party over a weekend, if you like, and introduce you to everyone. But for now, well, I am Matilda, this is Paul! Our baby, Eric, is sleeping, but you shall see him tomorrow. And these two are Matthew and Gwendolyn. They are Natalia's children. Natalia is Elena's-oh dear, you will never get it that way. There's too many! Let's make it gradual. Just Matthew and Gwen and us, for now. The rest, we'll worry about later."

"Thank you, Matilda, I'm very grateful. Also for the wonderful way you have received me."

"Well, it's as you said-we are all family!" And with that, Paul got up and said, "Matt and Gwen, perhaps you should say good night to cousin Arabella, then go up to bed-it is quite late."

The countess rang the bell. A servant entered. "Please show Miss Arabella to the Blue Room."

Then turning to her new cousin-in-law, the countess said, "Now, my dear, you go to bed. It's late, and we'll discuss this in the morning."

And after Matilda's words, the entire household said their good nights, and retired for the night.

14

Castle Colbert (1445)

T HE weekend party was in full swing-the castle rang with the voices of various people, yet it was all only the Carrington-Greys, and its extended family members of Staffords, Mowbrays, Albrights, Gwynds, and Treaves-all of whom had some of the Carrington-Grey blood. Earl Paul was determined for his cousin Arabella to meet all of her family-she was, after all, just as much a member as any of them.

The evening had started out quietly, and Arabella was very nervous. She was quite sure, that owing to the truth behind her birth, she would not be accepted. Matilda told her to relax. "Stop it, Bella! These people are, after all, your family. If any of them don't accept you, you are better off. You wouldn't want to associate with such folk, anyway. But I have a good feeling about this. And you know that Paul and I love you already."

Arabella hugged the younger woman. "Thank you, Mattie. Without you and Paul, I wouldn't have got past this week."

And now, sitting back in a corner for a few moments, Arabella went over everything and every initial meeting in her mind.

The first person she met, was her direct cousin, young Nadia Ecks. Nadia's father, Edward, was Arabella's mother's twin. Nadia, a lovely young woman of twenty four years, much resembling Arabella, ran up to her cousin, and gave her such a hug, as to almost knock her down. "Oh! I am so glad to finally meet you! We are going to be the best of friends! Papa! Come and see her!"

Nadia's father, Edward Ecks, came sedately up to his niece. "Well met, my dear. You are the image of your dear mother, my twin. How I wish she were here, too. What foolishness of her to stay away all these years. No matter what others may think, or feel, this family will never act in the way society tells them. We will not turn on our own. We come from Carrington-Grey stock, and self-protection is our motto. Welcome home. This is my wife, your aunt, Lady Francesca." A tall, thin woman with a warm smile came forward and gave Arabella a warm hug.

After that, all the family came rushing in and each one introduced themselves, and tried to remember their relationship to her. Arabella felt it was going to be difficult to remember them all-at the moment, the names were a blur, but she would eventually. Two people that stood out in her mind, were Edward Ecks, because he was her mother's twin. The second person was Lady Elena Stafford. Lady Elena was Edward's cousin, and was only one year his senior.

She hugged Arabella very closely, and sat down beside her. "We are so glad you've come, my dear. Edward is right-family stays together. Isabella should not have kept you away from us. But, all that's neither here nor there. It's water under the bridge, as they say. Now, we plan for your future!"

"I bet you know a lot of the people from the early days around here. Sorry! I didn't mean for that to sound the way it does."

Laughing, Elena replied, "That's quite all right, love. Yes, you are just so anxious for family, poor thing, you want to soak it up, don't you? Well, yes, I am the first grandchild of the first Earl and Countess. As a result, I saw a great deal-sometimes, more than was good for me.

"I knew your grandmother-Ann-Marie, her name was. My father's sister. And your grandfather, Jon, of course. There was also Maddelena, the youngest sister. And Anitra-she was Thomas' grandmother. And of course, their parents-who were my grandparents-the Earl and Countess. They are all dead now. My early days are so much different from now-the people, so different. Ah, dear, forgive me. Just mentioning their names make them alive for me, but only fleetingly. I'm going to leave you for a moment. You mingle with your cousins." And with that, Lady Stafford got up and left the room.

Arabella walked into the main hall, where most of the family were. She decided to walk towards Natalia Albright, Lady Elena's youngest daughter. Her initial meeting with Natalia was not a successful one. Matilda had warned her of the woman's bitterness with her mother, and how that had rubbed off in her marriage and her feelings towards her children. "Hello, Cousin Natalia! I can't tell you how much I've enjoyed talking to Matthew and Gwendolyn. They are such clever children. You must be proud." She saw at once she had made a mistake.

Natalia looked at this new family member. "Yes, they are good children, I am told. I receive good reports of them from Matilda and Paul-that is what matters. Matthew is learning well enough, so that he will be a very good squire of Henley House."

Arabella tried not to gasp. How cold was this person-and how very different from her mother, Elena!

Excusing herself from the frigid atmosphere surrounding Natalia, Arabella walked toward another group. Here she saw Anthony, Lord Stafford, Richard Stafford-two of Lady Elena's sons, and Clifton Treaves. The three young men were standing together, laughing and talking. Clifton saw Arabella coming. "Cousin Bella! Let me get you a glass of wine!" True to his word, the young man was off, before Arabella could say yay or nay. It meant something to her that people were calling her a nickname-it implied familiarity-and she needed that, after a lonely childhood. As much as she had loved her mother, she had kept her from all this.

After Clifton came back with her wine, he said, "I was telling these two chaps about my horses. I love them-and I've been breeding them, with the help of my father. Now, we've gotten to the point where we are one of the country's finest horse breeders. I will gift you with one-a cousinly gift-only the best!"

"You're going to gift her, and you're making us pay?" Anthony asked, in mock tones.

"Yes, I am. Anne and Riana have to eat-and so must I, for that matter!" The three young men laughed, with Arabella joining them.

She heard another voice-a new one, bellowing, "Here I am!" as it's owner followed. She smiled, as she saw the owner of the voice. Here, surely, was another cousin. Some here were distant, some closer, like Nadia, but they were all related to a degree somewhere. The young man with the booming voice had fiery red hair and warm brown eyes, that lit up when they turned towards her.

He walked towards her, bent forward to kiss her hand, and said, "You, I believe, are the cousin we are all honouring tonight. Allow me to introduce myself. My name is Trenton Mowbray. I, too, am a cousin-a prerequisite for this party, so Paul tells me! And your name is Miss Arabella Ecks. Well met!" And flamboyantly, Trenton bent down in a low, exaggerated bow.

Arabella looked at this young man. One could not help but like him-he seemed to be always laughing-his smile was engaging, and he was charming.

"Looked long enough?" he asked her.

Blushing furiously, Arabella begged his pardon, and started to walk away, but she felt his hand gently hold her's.

"I'm sorry," Trenton said, softly. "I didn't mean to embarrass you. I sometimes do spit things out-I'm told my mouth goes faster than my brain."

As she smiled at this, he said, "There, I hope I'm forgiven." Then, bending down a little closer, he said, "You may have stared enough, but I have not-we are not that closely related-beware cousin." And with a smile, he was off, leaving Arabella to stare after him, and to wonder why her heart was beating so rapidly.

As Trenton walked away, Nadia came forward. "I was watching the two of you," she gushed. "I think you two have the beginning of something special-I can see it in your face-and his."

"That's nonsense!" said Arabella, but not very convincingly.

"You know, what I think you feel for Trenton, is what I feel for Peter Carrington-Grey--you know, Paul's nephew. I know we are all cousins here, but in varying degrees. There has been some inter-marriage before, and I don't see why there can't be again-so long as the degree of relation is not too close. And our family is wealthy enough to buy a papal dispensation."

"Do you mean it?" Arabella felt very much lighter. Cousin Nadia had definitely read her feelings correctly. "I'm so glad you feel the same way for Peter!"

Nadia smiled. "Yes, isn't it wonderful? The only person both of us have to ask permission from-after my father for me-is Paul, since he, as the Earl, is the nominal family head. After that, a dispensation, which will be easy."

"Yes, I see that, but Nadia, you've overlooked one big hurdle: neither of them have proposed!"

"Fear not, Bella dear. They both will!" and with that, the two cousins linked arms and walked down the hall to join the party.

15

The Laurels (1555)

REED Mowbray leaned casually against the table, with his arms folded across his chest. "Come on, man, what do you say?" He asked the other occupant of the room.

Arthur Carrington-Grey sat on a chair, with his legs sprawled out. The very comfortable, easy way he sat in his cousin's house, spoke of the deep friendship between the two. This friendship had always been there, but eight years ago, certain events in life had cemented that relationship to something akin to love. The two were almost inseparable. They were very close in age-Reed was twenty-five, while Arthur was twenty-nine.

"I don't know, Reed," replied Arthur. "Perhaps I should think about this carefully."

Reed smiled. How careful Arthur was! A perfect foil for him-for he was rushing head-long into everything. How often Vicky, Reed's wife, told them that Arthur was Reed's life-saver.

The topic under discussion was Arthur's daughter, Mina. For Arthur, the world shone out of Mina-she was his jewel-his one prized possession-and only reason for being.

Ten years ago, Arthur, who had a penchant for travel, decided to set sail for India, a land he had always found fascinating. He was gone for six months. When he returned, the family was very surprised to find he didn't come back alone. He brought back a young Indian woman-his wife, he said. Arthur loved Samaira beyond any woman he had ever seen-she was strikingly beautiful to look at-long, lustrous black hair, and coal-black eyes. The family was scandalized, but Arthur's brother, the Earl, said the marriage was to be honoured. Samaira learnt English ways, and the English tongue very quickly, and the family started coming around to accepting her.

Then, it was announced that there would be a baby. Arthur was all a-flutter with excitement, and he and Samaira planned this new change in their life together. When the day came, the baby was born, but at the cost of her mother's life. Arthur couldn't believe he had lost her-he felt all the light had gone out of his life. Then the midwife brought him the baby and put her in his arms. He fell in love with this new chance at loving something. Samaira came alive for him again.

The first people to see him were Reed and Lady Victoria. Although Arthur appointed wet nurses and nannies for the baby, Vicky came often to cuddle the child, and very often, he and Mina went to The Laurels for the weekend. And so, Arthur's closeness with the Mowbrays grew.

What Reed was now proposing was for Mina, who was now eight years old, to go to Colbert Castle for the continuance of her education. It was a Carrington-Grey family tradition that all children of the family spend some time at the main family seat for their education. So far, Arthur had held back.

Reed came up to him, "Arty. Of all of us, you are the last person to hold back-after all, you're Charlie's brother."

"I know. It's just that Mina's all I have-I would like her to remain at home with me for awhile. What's wrong with keeping her governess, and having her educated at home?"

Before Reed could reply, his wife came up to Arthur and said, "You're not doing your daughter any favours by keeping her self-ishly with you. She needs the proper education, and she will only get this up at the castle. And although I know you adore her and want to keep her with you, I think we all know that is not your true reason for keeping her away from the castle. It's Jacquelyn, isn't it?"

Arthur bent his head, "Yes, it's Jacquelyn." His brother, Charles, the Earl of Easterbrook, was nine years his senior, and he and his wife, Lady Jacquelyn Devereux, had been married many years, but Arthur found it very difficult to accord the Countess the respect her station decreed. As a sister-in-law, Arthur detested her. Reed's wife, Lady Victoria, was affectionately called 'Vicky' by the whole family-her easy friendliness, familiarity, and genuine caring, made this lady an immediate family favourite. However, Charles' wife, Lady Jacquelyn, had never been called anything but 'Jacquelyn' by any member of the family. Her very personality made it impossible for anyone, including her husband, to call her 'Jackie.'

It was also Jacquelyn, of all the family, who resented, nay, hated, Samaira, and felt there was no room for such a person in the noble family of Carrington-Grey. She was very angry when her husband decided to accept Samaira, and acknowledge the marriage between her and his brother. It, therefore, was not surprising that Arthur would not care for his daughter to be in the home of a woman who had once hated her mother.

"Arthur. Whatever Jacquelyn thinks, has thought, or will think, Charles is the Earl, and he is a very forceful one. He has over-ruled her many times. Mina will not suffer in the house. Look, I must show you this." And Vicky extracted a letter from the pocket of her gown.

"It's a note from Charles to me," she said, when Arthur did not take the note. "In it, he has asked for you to go up to Colbert, with Reed and myself, if you wish it. We can discuss this with him. Come on, Arthur. You know Charles has always had your's, and Mina's, best interests, in his mind. Even though Jacquelyn is his Countess, he will not let her sway his mind as to his course of actions."

"Alright, I'll go," replied Arthur, just as there was a bombard of giggles and laughter as Mina came running into the room, with her two cousins. Reed's and Vicky's daughter, four-year-old Arabella, with vivid red hair, looked just like her father-who was a throw back to his ancestor, Trenton Mowbray. Her brother, the year-old Michael, was dark like his mother, and already half asleep, as the nanny carried him in her arms, to be kissed good night by his parents.

"All that noise, and it was only you two?" Reed said, in mock surprise. Then, lifting one child, then the other, he threw each in the air till she screamed with joy.

"Now girls, go on to bed now. Tomorrow's another day to be faced." And the girls left, after receiving their goodnight kisses.

Reed thought of the beautiful child that was his cousin's daughter. "Arty, I keep forgetting how lovely Mina is-so like her mother-perhaps even lovelier. She's only eight, and look at her! When she's older, you will have trouble with the boys buzzing around her!" So saying, he laughed, but noticed Arthur didn't smile back.

16

Castle Colbert (1555)

SITTING in the grand sitting room of the castle, Arthur and the Mowbrays looked around. The influence of its current mistress was certainly all over the room. Lady Jacquelyn Devereux, on her marriage to the Earl, brought back many period pieces from her homeland, and made to replace almost all of the old furnishings with her own, until she was stopped-by the Earl himself. He told her, that while he very happily welcomed his wife to add her personality to the castle, he also said that each generation had put their stamp on it, too, and nothing should be removed, or destroyed. The castle was a very old, beautiful building, and each part of it represented the generations of the Carrington-Grey family.

Very soon, Charles Carrington-Grey, the current Earl of Easterbrook, came strolling into the room. He gave his brother, Arthur, a squeeze around his shoulders. He had always had a soft spot for Arthur. When he brought home his Indian wife, he, like the rest of the family, had been scandalized, at first. But after witnessing how happy the woman made his always-sombre brother, and after getting to know Samaira a little better, he could only give his blessings, and accept the lady whole-heartedly into the family. This had not sat well with his wife, but since he was the earl, there was nothing Jacquelyn could do about that.

And now, he wanted his niece, Mina, to come to the castle, and enjoy the privilege that all the children of the family enjoyed. To stay for awhile and get some education from the tutors of the castle. He knew that based on Arthur's feelings against Jacquelyn, this was going to be difficult to do-but for the child's sake, he must try. And because Reed and Vicky were so close to Arthur, he had them come along to this meeting.

"Charlie, what do you want me to say? I understand what you want, and really, what should be, but owing to certain situations, I cannot let Mina come here."

"Arty, do you hear yourself? You've always been a quiet chap, living in the past, and we all let you, because that was the way you liked it, and it hurt no one. But now, you are endangering Mina's chances-you know you are. I know what all this is about-we all do. You're basing whether she comes here or not-all on the fact that my wife did not like your's. In essence, that's it."

Arthur looked up. "Isn't that enough? Christ, Almighty, Charles. You're asking me to put my daughter in the hands of the woman who could make her life miserable-I won't do that."

The earl sat up in his chair. "Am I asking you to do that, Arty? No, I'm asking you to bring Mina here for her education-that is not the same thing as what you are saying."

As his brother looked up in confusion, Charles continued, "If Mina comes, I will be responsible for her. I will appoint a nanny, a maidservant, and her tutor-all who will be answerable to me-and me only. Jacquelyn will have no part or parcel in her care. And you-spend every weekend here, so Mina doesn't miss you. I've covered everything. You see, Arthur, Castle Colbert is the basis for educating all Carrington-Grey children-even the ones who have the family blood, but don't carry the name. Why should not the niece of the Earl be entitled to the same education?"

"Sounds good to me!" Reed had said nothing up until now, but to break tension, he bounded up out of his chair, toward the earl. "And, Charlie, when Arabella and Michael come here in a few years, all will be smoothed!"

"All is smoothed now, Reed," replied Vicky, looking at her husband affectionately. She clutched his hand. Only she knew how worried Reed had been about Arthur and Mina. Behind that charming, carefree manner, was a man who thought a great deal, but kept things covered from the outer world.

17

Castle Colbert (1555)

MINA was thoroughly enjoying her stay at the castle. At first, she was homesick, and missed her father dreadfully. But her uncle pointed out to her that her father would spend every weekend at the castle while she was in residence, and sure enough, every weekend, Arthur came, and Mina began to find that she was enjoying her stay. She looked forward to the weekends, when her father came, and she could tell him about her week, and her academic progress; but she also enjoyed the rest of the week.

She wasn't the only child being tutored at the castle, of course-there were her cousins, too. Her cousin, Edmund, the earl's older son, no longer lived in the castle-he was now eighteen, and, as Lord Bently, lived in Bently Manor. The second son, Paul, was seventeen, and was just finishing his studies. The youngest, a girl named Josselyn, was fifteen, and was ahead of eight-year-old Mina in studies, but she was a very kind girl, and helped her cousin when she got stuck with something.

Also being tutored were the Albright and Treaves children. As a result, the Colbert Castle schoolroom was filled with a lively, happy group.

In the evenings, at the dinner table, the children sat together, and ate their meals. After which, they had an hour's leisure in the drawing room with the Earl and Countess, at which time they could quietly talk to them, or play chess, or be at some other quiet pastime, before it was time for bed.

At some of these times in the drawing-room, Mina would look at the Countess, and find that the look the countess bestowed on her was not as warm as the look she gave the other children. Sensing instantly that the countess didn't like her, she wondered why-she had never done anything to annoy her, so far as she could remember.

One day, she requested an audience with the earl. He was in his private office, busy with some papers. Seeing his niece, Charles got up, bidding her enter. He closed the door behind him.

"What can I do for you, my dear?"

"Uncle, I feel Aunt Jacquelyn doesn't like me. She looks angry when she looks at me. Did I do something wrong, and how can I fix it? I want everyone to like me."

Charles looked at this child, only eight years of age, asking a question no eight-year-old should ask. Silently, he cursed his wife.

"Oh, my dear, I think you've imagined it." What else could he say? "What reason would your aunt have for not liking you? You're a delightful child-sometimes, people cannot help the way they look. One day, I, or better yet, your father, will talk to you about the family in general, and then perhaps, you will get closer to understanding. But right now, you needn't worry about anything. I love you, your cousins love you-your father definitely loves you. Good night, my dear. I'll see you tomorrow."

Mina walked away, kissing her uncle good night, knowing there were unspoken words between her and the earl, which must remain unspoken for some years to come.

18

Castle Pondshire (1555)

THE weather was very pleasant, the flowers in full bloom, while nearby, a babbling brook gurgled and churned merrily on its way. On the other side, on a chair set by a footman, sat Lady Gwendolyn Gwynds, née Mowbray, the current Duchess of Pondshire, looking at the beauty of the estate all around her. Gwendolyn, referred to as 'Dolly' by her family, never failed to imagine at the wonder of her circumstances.

Over a hundred years ago, the Pondshire dukedom had been lost to the Carrington-Greys, owing to the duke and duchess of that time having only daughters. As a result, the dukedom was passed to a distant Gwynds cousin. The current Duke, Lord Cedric, came to visit his ancestors' relations-the Carrington-Greys-and met Gwendolyn Mowbray-who was visiting her cousin, the Earl of Easterbrook. The two fell in love, and married, much to the delight of the Earl-the Dukedom was back in the family!

A stranger mate for Dolly could not be found. While she was whimsical, bubbly, highly-charged and funny, like her brother, Reed-the Duke was staid, proper, and grim. However, his face always lit up at the site of his wife-the marriage was a happy one-and now, with four children-Rosamund, Katrina, Richard, and Isabella-it was also a fruitful one.

Seeing the nurse at a distance, Dolly called out, "Bring me the baby!" The nurse smiled at this unlikely duchess. "Yes, my lady," and placed the year-old baby in her mother's arms.

"Oh, Isabella's growing so fast! But after four, no more babies for me! Let's concentrate on this lot!" And with a laugh, she asked the nurse, "How are the others? Are they good--well-behaved?"

The nurse looked at her mistress. The entire household was shocked when the Duke married this woman-she was so unlike what everyone's opinion of a duchess should be-although she came from a noble family. But after these years, everyone adjusted to her, and could easily see why the duke loved his wife so much.

"Bless me, my lady, they are like angels. Little Lord Pavis actually ate all his food without complaint, and his two older sisters did not bully him all day."

"Oh, lovely! Their father will be most pleased-as am I!"

A page boy came into the garden, walking towards Dolly. "A missive for you, my lady."

Dolly passed the year-old Isabella back to her nurse, and took the letter. "Why, it's from Vicky! How nice! That's a lovely lady my brother married." As she read her sister-in-law's note, Cedric walked

into the garden. There was a saying at Castle Pondshire: only Lady Dolly could make Lord Cedric smile. Sure enough, the staid, normally quiet duke smiled as he saw his wife read a letter. He still didn't know what feature of Dolly's made him love her so, he only knew that before he met her, his life was bleak-and now, he felt completely content.

Walking towards her, "Gwendolyn, what do you think of going for a walk around the estate with your husband?"

Dolly looked up. "Delighted, my lord!" and she got up, putting an arm on the Duke.

"What does your brother write?" asked Cedric, politely, as he spied the Mowbray crest on the letter.

"It's Vicky who has written-Reed will write only if his life depended on it-and even then, with great reluctance," she smiled. "Reed has never been one for keeping up with correspondence.

As a result, if he wants to know how I am, he makes Vicky write. But this time, she has written of her own accord. She writes that all is well. Let me see," she scanned the letter. "Little Michael is growing very fast-too fast, according to Vicky. Her Arabella is all laughter and smiles-refuses to take things seriously-like her father, I suppose. Ara is the same age as our Katrina. My goodness, what a difference in personalities! She's only four, but our Kat is so serious, I think she'll grow up to be a nun."

"Do not worry, my love. As a duke's daughter, she will marry-we'll find someone suitable for her. But, that is far away-as you say, she's only four years old."

"Mm, yes," Dolly scanned the letter further. "Vicky writes that she, Reed, and Charlie, between them, have finally persuaded Arthur to get Mina educated up at the Castle. My goodness-that was a feat. How they first got Arty to let Mina leave Grey Manor, even for a little while-let alone, leave it for Jaquelyn's abode, is beyond me."

"I still do not understand your family's feelings toward Lady Jacquelyn," said Cedric. "I realize she's a bit cool, and staid-but so am I, and I have always been treated well."

"Well, it is a given that Jaquelyn is that cool person you said she is. But it's more than that: you see, she never accepted Arthur's Indian wife-in fact, she hated her. I'm personally of the opinion that it wasn't just the fact that she was Indian-it was also that she was a strikingly beautiful woman. Apart from Jaquelyn's snob factor, she is riddled with pure jealousy. And Mina, well, she's just a child now, but she promises to be even more beautiful when she's grown, and Jaquelyn can't stand that-plus the fact she's half-Indian."

"Well, yes, I must admit, I was a little shocked about this lady-Samaira, is it? But she turned out to be a very nice person-Arthur, too. It is a shame some will not forget."

Dolly rolled her eyes. "Not 'some,' darling-just one--Jaquelyn. She's the only one. Luckily, Charlie is not bowled over by her. He loves her dearly, but he will not be ruled by her."

"As should be the case-no man should let a woman rule him," replied the duke.

Dolly looked at her husband-he was quite serious. "Except you and me, my love. Everyone here at the estate, and my entire family, all know that you spoil me shamefully-I get anything I want!"

Cedric gave his wife one of his rare smiles. "Well, my dear, that is because you are not Lady Jaquelyn!"

So saying, the unlikely pair strolled arm-in-arm around their grounds.

19

Grey Manor (1563)

M INA Carrington-Grey sat on a window seat, occasionally looking out the window, as she did her sewing. It was a rainy day. The warmth of the fire was very pleasant as she worked. Mina was now sixteen years old, and had exceeded everyone's prediction of her increasing good looks. She was an exquisite-looking young lady-her jet-black hair hung straight and long, down past her waist. Her coal-black eyes, nestling in her pretty, heart-shaped face, sparkled brightly. Her cheekbones were high, but not sharp, giving her features a foreign allure.

She had enjoyed her education at Castle Colbert, and had completed it two years ago. She was very happy to be home. She never wanted to leave Grey Manor-but she knew that was not possible. Or was it? She was such an alien in her own family. By now, she knew the history of her own parents, and finally, the riddle of why she looked so different from the rest of the family was solved. Also solved was the riddle of why her Aunt Jaquelyn did not like her. But she was not bothered-she had enough love from the family to make her feel secure. Maybe, she thought, no one would want to marry her because of her half-foreign heritage.

When she mentioned this to her cousin, Josselyn, the girl laughed. "Do you jest, Mina? You are so pretty, it will not be difficult to marry you off. So, don't think it won't happen."

That was some time ago-Josselyn, some seven years her senior, was now married to a knight, and even a mother now. She, herself, at sixteen, was still a maid, but she very much feared her cousin was right-it would not be for long.

Sometimes she worried about her father. Arthur never remarried. She once said to him, "Father, Mother died when I was born-sixteen years ago. You've been without a companion for sixteen years. You should remarry. You seem so lonely-a wife will be good for you."

Arthur held the hand of his daughter. "My child, thank you for your caring thoughts. I will never remarry. The feelings I had for your mother were-well, I can only say, superlative. Never will I find someone like her."

"You don't have to look for someone like her-you will never be able to do that. Just look for someone-a woman who will please you, and you will be able to love her in her own right." Mina advised him.

Arthur smiled. "How wise you've grown, my dear. But to be honest, I don't have any wish-and before you continue, I've had conversations on this subject with your Uncle Charlie-so, now you, and he, will simply have to get used to my answer: no."

And so, that was that. Mina knew her father would not change his mind-unless he met that 'special' person. And it seemed that was very unlikely, but she was willing to hope.

20

Maltreaves Place (1563)

S ITTING in his private office at Maltreaves Place, eighteen-year-old James, newly-made head of this branch of the Treaves family, sat writing a very difficult letter to his cousin, Charles, the Earl of Easterbrook.

Looking around him, James still thought of this room as his father's office, which it was, a few days ago. A few days ago, before events occurred, causing his whole life to change drastically. Plague swept the town, and insidiously crept its way into the Treaves' household.

Within three days' time, both his parents, his sister, Belinda, and brother, Jack, had all perished of the dread disease. How James was spared, he didn't know. And now, he was head of a family of one-himself. It took him some time to get over the shock, but he knew it was his responsibility to let Charles know. Also, there was the duty of marrying, to get heirs, to prevent the Treaves line from dying out. Coldly, he thought of possibilities. His mind was blank, but his cousin could help him there, too.

All around him, he heard the servants cleaning and sweetening the house. That's the only sound he heard. Usually, he would hear Belinda's singing, out of key, in the solar as she sewed. It used to annoy him, her singing voice, because she couldn't sing. And now he felt he would give anything to hear that sweet, out of tune, voice of her's. Along with his mother's, telling her to get on with her sewing. Belinda had never married, even though she was twenty-two. Her father kept passing up various suitors, saying they were 'never good enough.' Now, poor girl, she went to her grave a maid.

As for Jack, he was James' twin. Unlike what most people say of twins, Jack and James were completely unalike-their personalities were like day and night, but they complimented each other perfectly. Jack, being the older by two minutes, was the heir to the Treaves' estate, but alas, he was dead at eighteen. So, James, who, as the youngest, had never been taught to run an estate, suddenly found he was the head of one.

Coming out of his reverie, James resumed his letter. He decided that he would also ask the earl's advice about estate running, and perhaps ask if he would be so kind as to send a factor who would help him. And the young man, who at one time lived only for pleasure, bent to write, and as he wrote, the heavy cloak of responsibility eased onto his young shoulders.

21

Bently Manor (1563)

Lady Elizabeth Carrington-Grey, née Calaigh, Baroness Bently, twisted her fingers together as she saw the nurse take her six-year old son, Brandon, for a much-needed wash.

Elizabeth adored her son, and very much wished she could care for him fully herself, without benefit of staff. It was pointed out to her, that as future Countess, this could not be-it simply wasn't done. Elizabeth wished she could set her own precedent.

When she mentioned this to Edmund, he only laughed and said, "Come on, my love! This only leaves you more time for me!" She smiled back-he was such a dear-she loved him so much-and she knew Edmund loved her-they were truly a lucky couple-much akin to the Duke of Pondshire and his Duchess, whose love was still going so strong after so many years.

"Well, Brandon will be ready soon, then we will be ready to go."

"Good," replied Edmund. "I don't know why my father has asked us, but he said it would be a good thing-any further details, must wait till we get there."

"Alright. I'll go check on Brandon." And with that, the Baroness left the room. Edmund smiled. The nurse was fully capable of getting the child ready and bringing him down, as she well knew. His wife was such a homebody-he firmly believed Elizabeth would be happier if they were peasants, and she could raise any a dozen children. Except, he thought, his wife did like her luxuries! And with a little laugh to himself, the happy-go-lucky Lord Bently went up to check on his wife and son.

22

Castle Colbert (1563)

CHARLES Carrington-Grey read the letter he received two days ago. He had read it many times-he knew it by heart, perhaps, subconsciously, he was wishing that by reading it many times, the wording would change. He felt so bad for James. He had already sent a message to his young cousin. Now he sat, waiting for his son and his family.

As he read, Jaquelyn came gliding into the room. "I do feel bad for poor James. Is there something we can do?"

"Of course, there's something," replied Charles, somewhat irritably. His wife always made a show of caring, and at times, she did, but only to an extant. Deep down, she ran cold; she always had. The only flash of passion he had ever detected in her was jealousy.

"Lord and Lady Bently, my lord, my lady." After allowing the young couple in, the steward left the room.

"Hello Pater!" Edmund walked briskly to his father. Turning to his mother, he murmured more sedately, "Hello, Mother."

"Hello dear," replied the Countess.

Six-year-old Brandon moved into the room with his mother, and there followed an exchange of greetings.

Finally, when things had quieted down, Edmund asked, "Well, Father, what's all this about? You and mother look well, no one is sick, are they?"

"Read this letter," and the earl put the letter into his son's hand.

"Oh my God! His whole family!" Edmund passed the letter to his wife. "In one sentence, he's asking us to look for a wife for him, in another, he's asking about getting help for the estate. Poor fellow, grief is making him think unclearly."

"Not at all. I think he's thinking as he should. Naturally, after the shock and sadness, he should be thinking about getting married and an heir." This, from the Countess.

Following the pained silence all around, Charles cleared his throat and replied, "I've already penned a note to him, asking him to come. I think there are things to be discussed that cannot be discussed in writing. He should be here in a day or two. And, Jaquelyn, when he comes, please, no pestering the poor boy about marriage plans--unless he mentions it himself."

23

Castle Colbert (1563)

A RTHUR and Mina walked into the drawing room of the castle. Both were surprised, yet pleased, to see Edmund and his family there. Also sitting in the room, was James Treaves. Charles had already told his brother the news, and Arthur went over to the young man to offer his condolences. Mina sat down, feeling inadequate. What could she say? She felt terrible for James-she had spent five years of her childhood in this castle, along with James. The two of them had studied together, laughed together, and fought together, along with the other children. She looked up at him-at the same time he looked at her. The sympathy in her limpid, black eyes told him all that was needed to say.

"What can we do for you, James," said Arthur. "Anything-anything that needs doing, we will do."

"Well, Uncle Arthur, Uncle Charlie, there are several things. Firstly, I don't know anything about running an estate. Can you teach me, Uncle Charlie-or Uncle Arthur? Edmund, you could teach me, couldn't you?"

Poor thing, he sounds so bewildered, thought Charles, and before he, or anyone could reply, James continued, "And also, I've been thinking. I'm the sole Treaves now. I need to marry, and quickly. Perhaps Aunt Jacquelyn, or Elizabeth, could help there?"

"Well, my dear, if you must know, I was the only one who felt you know exactly what you are saying. I will think of some candidates, and we will discuss this further." After this statement, the Countess excused herself from the room.

"I suppose that, uh, is a good thing, isn't it a good thing, Father?" Edmund leaned forward.

"And I will go over certain estate practices with you, and I'll send back two of my most trusted factors with you, to help you establish yourself," replied the earl, not quite answering his son. "Now, it is getting a bit late; shall we retire to face all this tomorrow? And don't worry, son. We're your family, and we'll look out for you."

As everyone stood up, starting to leave, the earl put his arm on his brother's. "Not you, Arty. Let's talk. In my office-we shan't be disturbed."

As the two brothers got comfortable in the earl's inner sanctum, Charles opened the topic in his mind. "We are here to discuss poor James' problem, and we will go over that; we'll help him as a family. That is what Carrington-Greys do. But other problems arise, brother, that must be faced and met with equally.

"I am referring to Mina. Lovely Mina is now sixteen years of age, and it's high time we looked for a husband for her. Now, don't cut up rough!" As he saw his brother's expression change.

"You can't keep her up at the Manor forever. Think of Samaira. Would she want her only daughter living out her life as a maid? I think not. We are a wealthy, well-connected family, and we'll use those connections to find her a man that's worthy of her. Now what do you say?"

"I think you're right." Whatever Charles had expected, he hadn't expected his brother to come up with an agreement so quickly.

Arthur elaborated, "She needs a place of her own."

"Yes, she does," said Charles. "And you're still young. You could still marry, and have a son to inherit the Manor."

Arthur held up his hand. "I've had this conversation just recently with Mina, and it appears every time I come here, I have it with you. I-will-not-marry.

"Grey Manor will go back to the Carrington-Grey inheritance for the second son. And if you keep bringing up this topic, I will stop coming here!"

The Earl smiled. "Alright, brother. You win." Charles had expected only to do battle over Mina.

The two men stood up. "Well, tomorrow, we'll work on James' problems, the day after, we'll start with Mina. You'll stay a few days?"

Arthur nodded. Rising from their chairs, the two brothers walked out the door.

24

Castle Colbert (1563)

THE next day, the family went about their regular routine, agreeing to set a family meeting in the afternoon.

Out in the gardens, Mina, James, Edmund, and Elizabeth, sat on chairs, discussing their lives in general. By a tacit agreement, all agreed to stay away from James' sorrowful situation-the topic was going to be broached later in the afternoon-so no one wanted to bring it up now. Edmund thought-let the poor devil forget for a little while.

They were listening to Mina, who was talking about her experiences in the castle with James. How they teased and fought. "You remember, James?" "Mina, surely, you didn't forget the time I beat you in the mathematics exam!"

With her chair off a little to the side, Elizabeth sat, half of her listening to the friendly banter around her, the other half playing with her son, Brandon. Brandon, at six, was not in the mood to stay in one place. He ran from his mother to his father, and James and Mina, receiving a hug and kiss from each person in turn.

Mina turned to look at Elizabeth, whom she liked very much. "You're such a good mother, Elizabeth."

Lady Bently blushed, and smiled. "Thank you, Mina. I wish I had a dozen children-and I wish I could look after them all myself-with no nannies-but alas, I can't, so I do what I can."

Edmund walked over to his wife, kissing her fondly. She really was the sweetest thing. He knew his mother thought Elizabeth's behaviour crass and unseemly, most inappropriate for a Baroness. Elizabeth knew how the Countess felt about her, but neither she, nor Edmund, cared. Lady Jaquelyn could not say anything, because Elizabeth came from nobility herself-it was just her behaviour. She once mentioned to her daughter-in-law that there were certain things she should not show-such as her emotions. Elizabeth felt that as she had given way for her child to be looked after by nannies, she was not going to be told not to show love to her son. Edmund had often told her he wished his mother had shown love to him and his siblings-but she was cold. As a result, while he and his siblings could joke and laugh with their father, they were very formal with their mother. Even Brandon, Elizabeth realized, was formal with his grandmother-there was no playing with Jaquelyn, while Grandpa Charles adored his grandson, and showed it.

Everyone in the garden was quietly talking and ruminating, and playing with Brandon, when a servant came. Addressing Edmund, he said, "It is time for the meeting, my lord. His Lordship, the Earl, requests everyone's presence in the drawing room."

The group stood up, walking back towards the castle. Mina walked over to James, giving his hand a squeeze. "Everything will be alright, cousin. As Father and Uncle said last night, we are family, and we are all here to support you. Now come-let's get this done." And with her arm linked in her cousin's, the two walked into the drawing-room with the others.

Elizabeth called for Brandon's nanny, who had made the journey with them. When the woman arrived, the Baroness reluctantly handed her son over, and followed the others into the room.

The Earl had papers in his hand. "Here, James. I have some written instructions regarding estates. Also, I have appointed two of my best factors-Ned Wilson, and Ralf Pinter. They will go back to Maltreaves Place with you, and help you set things aright. Keep both for as long as you wish. When you feel secure, one of them will come back-Ralf will stay and be your factor."

"Oh, thanks, Uncle." Although Charles was in fact James' cousin, because of the age difference, he gave him the respectful older title.

"And now," continued James. "If I could have some assistance regarding picking a wife."

"James! I know we have spouses picked, but you're being a little cold about it, don't you think?" Edmund had to say it.

"I don't think so, cousin. I need to be married, and soon. I'm the only Treaves, and I don't want the name to die out. Yes, I realize it sounds cold-it is, but I can't help it."

Lady Jaquelyn had been quiet up until now. She spoke up, "I have been going over several names, if you would like to-"

"No, Aunt. Just pick the one you think is most suitable-I'll marry her. The other way will take too long."

"Oh James." Elizabeth's soft voice could be heard. "You don't really want to do that, do you? Why not see a few girls-you have the opportunity?"

"Sorry, Elizabeth. It must be this way."

Clearly, they weren't going to change his mind.

Jaquelyn sighed, and said, "Well, the most suitable is the Honourable Veronica Talbot. She comes from a good family, and she's a decent girl."

"Good, she'll do." James smacked his palms together. "Uncle, can we get the contracts drawn up, as soon as she is informed-assuming she'll accept, of course."

"I'm glad you're giving her the opportunity to accept," muttered Edmund.

Mina was silent. She knew that the subject of her upcoming marriage was coming. Last night she saw her father and uncle go to the office after everyone left, and she had a very good idea what the topic of their discussion was: her marriage. Ah, well, she knew it couldn't be helped-there was no use fighting it-she had faith in her relatives to join her with someone she at least got along with. Love was too much to hope for-the love she heard her parents had for each other was not to be found a second time in one lifetime. The love between Edmund and his wife was wonderful, but love in contracted marriages was rare-cousin Edmund was the exception.

She worried about James. She had a feeling that his marriage would be loveless because he was entering it like a grand duty of procreation to keep the name going. It could even be one of dislike. Oh, hopefully, he and his wife found sympathy with each other, and that led to liking, and maybe, love.

25

Castle Colbert (1563)

THE Honourable Veronica Talbot, now Veronica Treaves, sat on one of the chairs of the drawing-room. She felt a little bewildered, and happy, at the same time. She was bewildered, because even though it was a very small wedding-due to the groom's recent bereavement, there were still a lot of personalities, with names to tack on to each one.

And she was happy, because the moment she had set eyes on the young man who was to be her husband, she had fallen hopelessly in love with him. She knew the reality of everything-the reasons why he was marrying her. He had sat with her privately and told her everything. "So, you see," he ended. "This is a very cold situation, and you don't have to accept it." Then, even he felt he owed her a little bit more, so he said," And if you do, I'll try to be a good husband, and who knows where our relationship may take us?" Then he smiled at her.

Veronica had smiled back, and said, perhaps too forcefully, "Oh, no! I'll be happy, no, honoured, to be your wife, and I can only hope I don't disappoint you."

To which James replied, "I'm sure you won't." And she had felt all warm inside, as if being enveloped by a large blanket.

Looking around her now, Veronica looked at her new family. At the Earl, whom she liked, and his wife, whom she didn't. Then came the Earl's brother, Arthur-she liked him, too. When she saw Arthur's daughter, Mina, she felt intimidated, even though Mina was a very nice, kind person, and had welcomed her to the family with great warmth. She was so beautiful! Veronica, herself, had never been even a little pretty. Her most attractive quality were her eyes-they were a lovely almond shape, and were clear grey. Lady Bently was also a very lovely woman-dark-haired and brown eyes--and she was so petite-she looked rather adorable with the very tall Edmund.

The women of the family were certainly very lovely-but they were also very kind-with the exception of the Countess. They made Veronica feel right at home.

Little Brandon was adorable, too, copying the adults in welcoming her to the family. She smiled at everyone, but secretly wished she could be alone with her husband.

As if he had heard her thoughts, James came up to her. "We are making an early start for Maltreaves Place tomorrow. Therefore, I suggest we retire for the night." And giving his wife his arm, he prepared to lead her out of the room.

Mina ran up and caught up to them. "I won't see you tomorrow-I shall be sleeping in! But I'll see you soon."

Good-nights were spoken all around, and the newlyweds left the room.

26

Castle Colbert (1564)

Mina sat looking at the young man before her. She could not believe she was married to him. How did she feel about it, truly? Well, as far as rank went, her uncle and father had found her a duke! As for the man, himself, Geoffrey Gaines was a handsome, charming, man, but Mina felt he had an extremely exaggerated sense of his own importance. So, as she had thought the year before-yes, her marriage had pushed her up in the world, but she did not expect to be very happy in it. She only hoped her husband was kind. He was a conceit, she could see that-but he could be kind-she hoped and prayed that he was.

Geoffrey Gaines, the Duke of Ainsleigh, looked at his bride. Sitting in all her wedding finery, his newly-made Duchess looked like something out of this world. Her long black hair hung down her back, showing her virgin state. Geoffrey couldn't believe this beautiful, precious being was his. He knew the story of her parentage-the Countess had told him. However, he did not care. As far as he was concerned, it was that mixed parentage that made her the beauty she was today. He looked at her uncle and father, along with her other family members. He was on his best behaviour tonight-all charming, but somehow, he felt his new wife read him correctly. Ah, well, it hardly mattered. The fact was, he, too, needed to marry and provide heirs; love was not in the equation. She just needed to do her duty to her new family. If she did, they would get along. If she didn't-well, he would think about that another time.

But he read Mina to be smart. She may not be happy about the situation, but she would do everything expected of her.

Sitting on another chair in the room, Lady Jaquelyn sat, trying not to show her true feelings. It was absolutely galling to know that the one child she had trouble getting to like-because of her mother-now outranked her. Grudgingly, she admitted the girl looked beautiful in her wedding clothes. Sighing deeply, she put a smile on her face, and looked part of the crowd, trying to show enthusiasm.

Also in the room, was James Treaves, and his wife, Veronica. The two came over for the wedding with their new baby, Aidan. Aidan was only a few months old, and was born into the world with much relief from both his parents.

Very shortly after their marriage, Veronica continued to hopelessly love her husband, but James could not return it. He could not forget why he got married in the first place, and waited for a baby.

When Aidan was finally born, Veronica felt that now, perhaps, James would feel something akin to love for the woman who was his heir's mother, but this was not to be. They were just too ill-suited. Veronica was not James' idea of the wife he would want-too late, he realized that he should not have rushed into it-he should have taken his family's advice, but that was not possible now. He was always civil and kind to her, but Veronica knew there was no love, and this knowledge turned her bitter. She had thought it would be enough to just marry James, and be with the man she loved, but she found that love unreturned, made one very unhappy, indeed.

In one corner of the room, Arthur stood, looking at his daughter. Feeling his eyes well up, he heard a voice behind him. "Don't let her see you do that."

Always there in his time of need, Reed linked an arm around his cousin and dear friend. "You'll upset her. Show her you're happy."

Arthur smiled. "Thank you."

"No problem. You'll do the same for me when it's Arabella's turn."

27

Ainsleigh Hall (1582)

L᠎ADY Mina Gaines, née Carrington-Grey, Duchess of Ainsleigh, came rushing down the stairs of her lovely home, which, though styled Hall, was really a castle. Mina had never learned to walk sedately as a duchess should, but had gone running or rushing, same as she did when younger. And now, at thirty-five, nothing had changed. She had done her duty-she had given the family the long-awaited heir, along with two daughters, so her husband never bothered her about her strange, sometimes unladylike ways.

Walking into her special withdrawing room, that her husband had had designed for her, she sat down to relax for awhile. The room was cozy, with lovely furnishings, and she loved it. What she didn't like was the profusion of mirrors in it. Geoffrey had seemed to think she enjoyed looking at her image all the time. He certainly enjoyed watching himself-his vanity had never stopped-possibly, it had increased with age. When he sometimes sat here with her, his eyes were on the mirrors, even while he was talking to her.

She found his vanity and conceit quite disgusting, but she put up with it. It was a small price to pay for all she had: for one, the beautiful home and position. But the main thing was her children: she absolutely adored her children, and found, to her amuse-ment, that as far as they were concerned, she acted very much like a duchess in wanting the best possible marriages for them in the future.

Her firstborn, Mason, the long-awaited heir to the Gaines fortunes, was the pride of her existence. At seventeen years of age, he took just after her: thick black hair, and coal black eyes, indicating a throwback to his grandmother, Samaira.

Her second child, was sixteen-year-old Abigail, a lovely girl with coils of thick, golden hair, and bright blue eyes.

Finally, her youngest: Olivia, who, at only twelve years of age, showed signs of great beauty with features and colouring just like her mother and grandmother, Samaira.

All in all, Mina had to admit, that although the beginning of her marriage was unhappy, once the children came, she found some joy in her situation. Added to all that, she was a good chatelaine, and was well thought of and respected by all her staff. She had come quite a long way from her wedding day. The only blot in it all had been the death of her father two years ago.

Arthur's grandchildren had been his greatest joy, and he had been a frequent visitor at Ainsleigh Hall. But in later years, his health had started to fail, and it wasn't long before, one morning, his servants went into his chambers to wake him, but found, alas, he had died in his sleep.

Arthur's death had been a huge sadness to all the family. It wasn't long after that, that the Earl died, too. Lady Jaquelyn died the year before, and as cold as she was, Charles found he missed his wife of many years.

Now, all the older generation was gone. Edmund was the new Earl of Easterbrook, and Brandon was Lord Bently. He lived at Bently Manor with his wife, Deandra Bailey, and their three children, Michaela, Amira, and Nathan.

Thinking of all the changes that occurred in the family in the past few years, Mina picked up some embroidery. As her fingers started expertly flying with the needle, in and out of the fabric, she looked up, and took a good look at herself in the mirror.

Putting down her work, she got up and walked closer to the mirror, staring at the image reflected. What she saw was a strikingly beautiful woman, not in the first flush of youth, but looking very good for her thirty-five years. Her jet-black hair, now piled high on her head in elaborate coils and twists, had not one strand of grey. Her figure, after three children, was still slim and supple. She knew she could easily hold her own amongst much younger women. With a little smile-realizing she had a vanity almost like her husband's-the beautiful Duchess sat down and returned to her embroidery.

Seeing his mother in her private sanctum, Mason Gaines, not for the first time, was spellbound by her beauty. He loved her deeply-everything about her. She was the kindest person he ever met. His father, though charming and seemingly caring, was a very superficial man. But his mother was genuine. If he had any hope, it was with his mother.

Clearing his throat to make his presence known, he walked in. Mina looked up. "Hello, my dear. Are you having a lovely day?"

"Yes, Mother, I am. I must talk to you."

She leaned forward. "I'm listening, Mason."

Mason sat down, rubbing his palms together. "Well, Mother, I met a girl. Please, let me finish," he said, as he saw his mother about to speak.

"I'm in love with her, Mother. And don't say I'm too young at seventeen. It does happen, sometimes. She's wonderful, Mother. You would like her. She's, oh, she's just perfect."

Mina looked at this jewel of her's. This child, who was the star and the future of the Ainsleigh name. He was so young. And unless the young lady in question came from at least an honourable household, there was no way he would be permitted to marry her.

Mason continued. "Her name is Ellyn Pole. She's wonderful-everything I could want."

"What about her family? You must realize by now, Mason, that if her family are not honourable, you will not be permitted to marry her. Your father will never allow it, and I, too, would have reservations. You're the heir to a dukedom. As terrible as it sounds, you will not be wasted on just anyone. I must find out more about this Ellyn Pole. Also, have her come to me-she can come in here-let us say, tomorrow past mid-day. After I have seen her, I will make my judgement, as to whether we can pursue this situation further and tell your father. That is all I can do, son. Just make sure she comes tomorrow."

And with that, the Duchess got up, and left the room, giving her son a fond kiss as she left.

28

Ainsleigh Hall (1582)

SIXTEEN-YEAR-OLD Ellyn Pole sat in the private sanctum of Mason's mother, the beautiful Duchess. She was awed by the older woman's beauty and poise. Looking around her at the equally beautiful surroundings, she looked back at the duchess, and smiled.

"Miss Pole? May I call you Ellyn?" Receiving a shy nod, Mina continued. "Ellyn, I'm sure you know why I want to meet you. I can see by your expression that you love my son, and that makes me glad, because he obviously loves you, too. Unfortunately, things are not that easy. Marrying the heir to a dukedom means, obviously, that one day, you will be a duchess. Therefore, I am sure you must be aware that such a person must be above reproach. She does not have to come from nobility, but neither can she be a peasant. Now, I am sure you're not a peasant, dear, but I do need to know a little bit more about your parentage."

Ellyn cleared her throat. "My lady, my father was a very simple man. He was, what you might call, a commoner-though not a peasant. But he married above his class-my mother was Eloise Drayton-from the middle class. And her mother's family descended from Roland, the Knight of Bansch. Mina had heard of the near-legendary Roland. She had also heard how his family had broken up and married into the lower classes. Perhaps this could be the chance to get old Roland's descendants back into the nobility, even higher than his own class? And in so doing, she would be granting her dearest child's wish. And she liked what she saw in the girl, Ellyn. It remained to talk to her husband.

"Thank you, Ellyn. You may wait in the other room. Mason will see you home."

After the girl had left the room, Mina said, "I like her, Mason. And before she got here, I did some research of my own. She really is descended from the Knight of Bansch. I am going to talk to your father. I'm sure there will be no trouble, once he hears of her antecedents-it will be another thing for him to brag about." Then, she realized she said the last part aloud, when she meant to only think it.

"Now see her home. I've got work to do." And as the young man left the room, Mina walked across the room to the connecting door, which led to the Duke's private office. "Perhaps I'll be a grandmother by the end of next year!" was her last thought, as she sat down to talk to her husband.

29

Maltreaves Place (1582)

THE years had been kind to Veronica Treaves. As a young woman, she had been plain, but as the years advanced, the mousy brown hair turned grey, giving her a distinguished look. And the earlier bitterness of her loveless marriage was replaced with a calm acceptance, thus giving her a dignified bearing. James, ever the gentleman, had continued to show her kindness and courtesy, as his wife and the mother of his children, but love had never blossomed in this poor marriage. She was by no means an old woman-in fact, her grey hair had come prematurely through her early days of stress. However, she was now at a point in her life where she could truly say she was content.

She almost smiled, as she thought of the last few days. She had heard, in a very roundabout way, of a woman her husband had been seeing. Remembering her feelings of anguish, betrayal, and pain, she sat down, going over everything. It was her faithful lady's maid, Gwennie, who told her everything. Gwennie told her about what she heard, regarding the master and another woman.

She even remembered going into James' study, sitting down, and saying, in as steady a voice as she could muster. "So, it is true that you are seeing another? May I at least know for how long?"

Looking up from his desk, James' face flushed, as he said, "I'm so sorry, Veronica. I had never meant for you to know. I didn't want to add to any worries for you. I'm going to be perfectly honest with you-if you want me to stop, tell me, and I shall."

Bracing herself for his confession, Veronica sat ramrod straight in the chair. "Continue."

James swallowed. "As you know, our marriage has always been a little, ill-suited, and it is all my fault. You have been a wonderful, loving wife and mother. I saw to it that you are treated with the respect you deserve.

"Things continued over the years-the children, the estate. I never thought to find physical happiness with a woman. But one day, as I was passing the village, I met a young woman-Martine Ainsworth, by name. Our relationship was fast, physical, and it was over in one month. The result, unfortunately, was Emma."

"A baby! You had a baby with another woman?"

"I'm so sorry, Veronica, I thought you knew the whole story. Well, yes, a baby. As I said, this is all over now. Martine and I are not seeing each other-it was over quickly. And there is no one else. It's all over."

Veronica stood up. "It will never be completely over if there is a child in the equation. How old is she?"

"Two months. She's two months old," muttered James.

"Well, I suppose it's a blessing she's a girl. She can not come back in twenty years' time, and lay a claim to Aidan's inheritance. And I'm glad you no longer are seeing her mother. You've never loved me, but I've been hopelessly in love with you from the moment we met. As long as it's just the two of us, I can learn to be content."

James hung his head. What could he say? No, he never had loved his wife, and he knew he never will-but he would continue to accord her the respect and courtesy she deserved.

Going over all of the events in her mind, Veronica smiled. Over all, she had handled herself rather well. She wanted to tell James that she wanted to kill his mistress and baby, but she had been dignified and serene, and she knew that James respected her more for that. It also put her at an advantage over him.

Aidan Treaves bounced merrily into the room. He had been fishing with a school friend, and was a little bedraggled.

Looking up, Veronica smiled at her son. She adored him. At eighteen years of age, Aidan had the misfortune to resemble his mother. This made him not a very attractive young man, alas. It might also account for the fact that he had never been close to his father. He knew very well about the relationship between his parents, or the lack of one. He knew he was only useful to his father in being the heir to the Treaves' name and estate. Other than that, there was nothing else. Such issues didn't bother him-he was too devil-may-care to worry about that.

Bending down to Veronica now, and kissing her on her cheek, "Hello, mother. When will luncheon be served? I must say, I'm famished!"

Smiling, Veronica replied, "Not for half an hour, dear. Go get cleaned up. By the time you're done, it shall be ready."

Bounding up the stairway, Aidan ran into his sister, Nadia. At fifteen years of age, Nadia was the image of her father, and the apple of his eye. According to James, his little girl could do no wrong. She adored him. Her relationship with her mother was cold and austere, since she knew her mother didn't care or approve of her.

What a family we are, thought Aidan. "Have you been fishing again?" Nadia questioned him.

"I should think that was obvious. Now excuse me, munchkin, while I go get washed and changed for luncheon."

Going into his rooms, Aidan closed the door, letting out a huge sigh. Alright, he was alone, he could stop pretending. Unbeknownst to his parents, he had overheard their conversation of a few days ago. He had felt rage at his father for betraying his mother. After thinking it over, though, he realized his father had never been unkind or cruel to her. It's true, he never loved her, but Aidan was old enough to realize that one could not force emotions. There was a servant girl here in the Manor who had proven that! But enough about Annie the maid.

What surprised him the most was the child-or baby. To think that his father had another child was something incomprehensible to him. To him, his parents were old, and past--THAT. Apparently, such was not the case. Well, he guessed he would never meet this mysterious Emma who was, after all, his half-sister. He rather thought he would like to, though it would never happen, at least not in his mother's lifetime.

Getting himself up out of the chair, Aidan Treaves dressed for luncheon hurriedly, then made his way down to the family, seated at the table.

30

Castle Colbert (1590)

Dowager Duchess, Lady Elizabeth Carrington-Grey, sat in the Earl's private office. She loved this room, the best of any other in the castle. One would not recognize this sad, lonely, middle-aged woman to be the same loving, motherly young woman of thirty years ago, but a great deal had happened.

Three years ago, she lost her husband, Edmund. He died from a very bad bout of illness. Heartbroken, their son, Brandon, took over the reins of the earldom. Then, another bombshell: Just a few months ago, Brandon's carriage overturned, and he and his wife, Deandra, were killed instantly. This left Elizabeth's twelve-year-old grandson, Nathan, as the Earl of Easterbrook. She sighed. How her world had turned. In just a short space of a few years, the Carrington-Grey family suffered loss after loss, and its leadership lay in the small, fragile hands of a twelve year old boy. And now, there was nothing left for her in this life, except to guide Nathan in his inheritance, and help him make the decisions that needed to be made. His sisters, too, were young, and husbands needed to be found for them. But as soon as Nathan attained adulthood, and the girls were married off, she was finished. She wanted to meet her Maker, and Edmund and Brandon, in heaven. She missed them so much.

Sitting back in her chair, the Dowager Duchess dreamed of the time she was a young bride, newly-come to this family, on the arm of her handsome, loving groom. How she loved Edmund. In her dreams, he came alive for her again.

31

Maltreaves Place (1598)

SIXTEEN-YEAR-OLD Emma Ainsworth looked up at the old manor house. A lovely old home, she thought, and so cozy-looking. *I don't even have a right to be here, but I really need to do this.*

Gathering up all her courage, she lifted up the heavy iron knocker, and knocked on the door. It was opened by a manservant who peered down at her. Looking at the simply-dressed, but seemingly well-bred young woman, he said, "Yes, miss?"

Emma cleared her throat. "Please, sir. I would like to speak to Mr. James Treaves, please."

The manservant looked at this young woman with more interest, and guessed her identity immediately. "I think, miss, I better take you to Mr. Aidan Treaves-Mr. James' son. Please follow me."

Stepping inside of the house, Emma looked around with interest as she followed the servant. They stopped before a door. The servant rapped gently, then opened it. "There is a young lady here, sir, whom I think you should have a conversation with." And so, the servant left them in the room, closing the door.

Aidan smiled inwardly. *Trust Ricks for that!* He was servant to Aidan's master, but Ricks had been his father's butler, as well. As a result, he often gave Aidan the benefit of good advice, stepping out of the master/servant realm.

Turning to look at the young woman before him, Aidan got a good look at her since she came into the room. His smile vanished, and his face drained of colour. "I think I know who you are," he said gently. "You're my half-sister, aren't you? Do you know how I knew that? You look just like our father. Please, sit down, and tell me about yourself. I'm Aidan, your half-brother, by the way, and I won't bite. I've been wanting to meet you for a long time."

Emma drew a deep breath. "My name is Emma Ainsworth, and yes, you guessed correctly-I am your half-sister. My mother always told me to stay away from my father's family, but now she's dead, I needed to satisfy my curiosity. So, I decided to come and visit my father. I didn't want anything-I just want to see him, and get to know him."

Aidan's face puckered. "Oh, my dear, I wish I didn't have to tell you this, but our father is dead. He died five years ago. I am very sorry."

Emma swallowed hard. Then she got up. "I am sorry, too. But I am so glad to have met you, Aidan. I better leave now. One thing my mother did say was that my father's wife would not appreciate my being under her roof, so I had better leave."

Aidan held her arm gently. "My mother is dead. She died two years ago. I live here with my wife, Selena, and she, as well as myself, will welcome you with open arms. I have mentioned you to her. You are free to live here with us for as long as you wish. And as my sister, I will help you find a husband. I have another sister-or rather, we do. Nadia, but she's married and lives very far away. So, I welcome your presence, my dear. Please stay. From the moment I knew of your existence, and that was when you were two months old, I longed to meet you. I thought that would never happen. Now you are here, you must make your home with us."

After his speech, the young master of Maltreaves Place rang the bell. Ricks the manservant came in. "Please ask the Mistress to come in. Tell her what we wanted has happened." And smacking his palms together, Aidan laughed. "You will bring joy to this house again, Emma! Would you believe, this house hasn't seen true happiness since my grandparents were alive? After our father took over, he never recovered from their deaths, and so his outlook on life was cold, bleak, and sad. My childhood was not the most pleasant. Selena has been my saving grace, and now there's you, my dear! What fun we shall have!"

And Emma saw, that although her half-brother was so much older than she was, in many ways, he was an innocent, and ever the cheerful optimist. She sat in the room, and stood up to meet and greet Aidan's wife, a beautiful young woman, who gave her a warm, sisterly greeting.

Yes, thought Emma. I could be very happy here. And leaving the last vestiges of her lonely childhood with her mother behind her, Emma prepared to face this next phase of her life, which promised to be more enriched, happy, and fulfilling.

32

Ainsleigh Hall (1667)

NINE-YEAR-OLD Lydia Gaines stood looking up at the massive portrait in the entrance hall. The face looking down at her had fascinated her ever since she was a very small child. She knew who it was: Lady Mina Gaines, a long-ago Duchess of Ainsleigh. She also knew the history. Lady Mina's husband, the Duke, had the huge portrait of his wife painted, because he was enthralled by her beauty. There was a portrait of him, too, but that did not get as much attention as the one of his wife.

Absently, she stroked her cheek, as she continued to gaze at the image. She had been told she resembled the old duchess. If such was the case, she was pleased, because the woman was the most striking she had ever seen. I hope I grow up to look just like her, she thought.

Suddenly, she heard a noise. Looking around quickly, she relaxed. It was only her brother, Henry.

"Are you looking at that, again? You don't look like her, you know. She was beautiful-you look like-well, like, ew." The ten-year-old boy ducked, as his sister aimed a potentially good smack his way.

"Children! Stop it!" Their mother, Lady Charlotte, could be heard as she came up to stand beside Lydia. "Please stop your fighting. I'm getting a headache. Now, I'm going to have a little rest, so that I'll be fresh for dinner. I suggest the two of you calm down, and work on something quiet."

As the children left the room, Charlotte looked up at the large painting. The face of Mina Gaines smiled back at her. Charlotte, who in all of her life had never been called even remotely pretty, looked at the picture with something akin to envy. How ridiculous, she thought. Now, I'm jealous of a dead woman. Addressing the painting, "You've passed your good looks down to my daughter, and for that, I am thankful." And turning, she left the room.

33

Colbert Castle (1667)

Lucas Gaines, the Duke of Ainsleigh, sat down at the desk with the Earl of Easterbrook. Anthony Carrington-Grey was only ten years of age-the same age as his son, Henry, but responsibilities had come very early to this young child, leaving him lonely and bewildered.

In the past few years, many direct members of the Carrington-Grey family had been wiped out, by disease, or other such calamities, except for Anthony. The family hung by a tiny thread. On Anthony's very young shoulders, rested the entire fortune and earldom, and as Lucas could see, the strain was getting too much.

Patting the young earl on the shoulder, Lucas said, "Don't worry, Tony. I will guide you all the way. I have already appointed factors for you. I'll come here regularly every week, to see that everything is handled properly. I will go over everything with you. You will not have to take up the full reins until you feel confident." Then realizing the earl was still just a boy, he said, "And you will have a lot of time to play-we will make sure of that. And the rest of the family will come-you won't be left alone. Not only that, the other children will be here in a few days, to take up their studies with you."

"Thank you, Uncle Lucas." The boy's shoulders visibly relaxed.

"And Mrs. Mindly takes good care of you."

At the mention of the housekeeper's name, Anthony smiled. "Yes, she was a wonderful nanny to me, and now, she's housekeeper. But she still treats me like a very small boy-I rather like that."

Lucas smiled. He had such a person in his childhood, too. "Yes, it's good to have someone who treats you as if you were still little. I believe we all need that."

As he got up, he put his arm around the boy, and felt the fragility of the lad. "Don't worry. It will all be fine. Now! Enough about business for now! I, for one, am famished!" And man and boy walked over to the beautiful castle verandah, where the servants had set out suitable refreshments.

34

Stafford Castle (1667)

MARK, Lord Stafford, lay in the arms of his favourite paramour in his private chambers. Yolande Laurent was a young woman with many charms, all of which had captivated the young earl. Not known for brains, Yolande had ample physical attributes; Mark thought to himself, as long as she doesn't talk, everything will be fine. At twenty-nine years of age, he was still unmarried, completely by his own wish. He just desired a life of what he referred to as amusement, entertainment, and gaiety. As a titled lord, he had the means, and the facilities, to see to his wants, and his good looks helped him with those of the female persuasion.

His family was beside themselves. As a titled lord, it was his familial duty to marry and beget heirs. At almost every gathering, the topic of his bachelor state always came up. "Oh come!" He'd reply to this. I'm having too much of a good time-time enough for that later." Smiling at that, now, he thought-and later may never come.

Stretching his arms out to their fullest, Mark looked out of the window. It looked like late morning, judging by the light. He had promised Lucas he would go down to Colbert Castle and help him out with tutoring Tony. Poor fellow!

Looking at the woman beside him, Mark suddenly felt a little revulsion. This happened all the time-maybe his family was right after all, and one woman for him was better, but honestly, he didn't know if he could make that kind of commitment. A little intelligent conversation in a bedmate was a good thing, and that was not possible with this one-although, thought Mark, she has a figure that I cannot seem to get enough of. Ah, well, a pity one can't have everything. "Get up, Yolande! Here!" He tossed her a few coins from the table by the bed. "Get yourself dressed, go to the kitchens and get something to eat, then you must go."

"I shall see you again tonight, my lord?" Making a quick grab for the coins, he noticed, the woman aimed a look his way. In its cheap prettiness, it served to disgust him further.

"No. I must go to visit my young cousin, and I'll be away for a few days."

With her black hair down her back, and one lock hanging down the front of her shoulder, Yolande stood with a sheet around her, swivelled her ample hips, and smiled invitingly. "Very well, my lord. I shall be here when you return."

"No, by God, you shall not!" When he saw Yolande's face, he lowered his tone. "No more, Yolande. Do you understand? It is not your fault, 'tis mine. I always do this-to myself, and to the women I'm with. I think it best that you do not come here anymore."

"My lord, I'll do better!"

Gently prying the prostitute's hand from his arm, Mark said, in as gentle a voice as he could muster, "Never beg, Yolande. That will definitely not help. Now please. Take your money, and get yourself a good meal. After that, as I said, you must go, and never come back."

"It's another one, isn't it? Or can you finally be thinking of marriage? We can still continue-marriage has never stopped other men."

Now Mark was angry. "It is no concern of your's what it is. If you do not leave now, I'll have you escorted out by my guards, and I do not want to do that. Get yourself gone, Yolande, and don't show your face to me again."

Never mind, he'll change his mind one day, she thought, then, quickly dressing, left the room. Mark drew a deep breath. Whew! The feelings of revulsion in him were increasing every time he was with any prostitute-but mainly with Yolande. Maybe it was time to settle down. How pleased his family will be, he thought. But let's go to young Anthony first, and deal with that.

And so thinking, Lord Stafford called his servants. He was going to have a large breakfast, and then he would go. But first, he was going to get his manservants to fill the large tub, so he could wash away the memories of the night before.

35

Castle Colbert (1667)

THE old castle was teeming with the voices of children, along with adults. Young Anthony looked around and thought, it's so nice to see everyone. And to have my lessons with my cousins, it's wonderful. Looking at his older cousin, Mark Stafford, Anthony smiled even more, and Mark smiled back. Of all his family, he practically hero-worshipped Mark, and Lucas was aware of this. That is why the Duke had Mark come down to give Anthony some aid. Mark had some bad habits, in fact, his way of life was reprehensible-no one could talk to him with any success. But his one saving grace was his great affection for his young cousin, and his willingness to help him.

Mark watched as the various younger members of the family gathered around Anthony after the dinner hour. All the family was sitting in the great drawing room of the castle. He smiled. It was rather nice, really. The children were all roughly the same age, given a year or two to three. They had always been close. He was enjoying himself, looking at them, listening to their banter.

Already, he felt more relaxed. The earlier feelings of disgust and revulsion had left him completely, and he knew that he would continue in his ways-no settling down for him! As soon as the negativity ended, so, too, ended his feelings of wanting a wife-until, of course, those feelings returned.

As he was sitting, Sarah Treaves came and sat next to him. "Hello, Mark." Of all the people in the family, Sarah, and Thomas

Mowbray's first wife, Lady Natalie, were always the ones bringing up the topic of his bachelor state. Since Thomas had set Natalie aside ten years ago, on the grounds that he did not have children with her, it was only Sarah that bothered him.

"Hello, Sarah. How are you and the family?"

"We're doing very well. In a minute, Charlotte will announce bed for the children."

Sure enough, Duchess Charlotte, acting as hostess for the household, said, in a loud voice, "Children, the hour is late. Say your good nights, and retire. We shall see you in the morning." After good nights were spoken, and the children left the room, Charlotte looked at Sarah conspiratorially.

Catching the hint, Sarah said, "I want you to come here for awhile." And getting up and taking Mark's hand, she prepared to lead him out of the room.

Perplexed, Mark laughed. "You're not going to take me for a secret assignation, are you, Sarah? Joshua is a strapping great lout, and I don't wish to be in a fight with him!"

Laughing, Sarah replied, "Joshua knows very well what I'm doing-as do they all."

Sarah took Mark to the great library. In the empty room, she waited with him. Before anything else could be said, Charlotte walked in, closing the door behind her.

"Well, cousin? I'm sure you must know why we're here," Charlotte smiled.

"Yes, of course I do, and I can only tell the both of you, to please stop this. I am not ready to marry-honestly, I don't know if I'll ever be ready, even with my responsibilities and such. However, it is definitely not now. So please, dear ladies, for heaven's sakes, for the last time-stop trying!" And with his hands in the air, Mark sat down heavily on the sofa.

"Yes, yes, we hear you, don't we, Sarah? But you need a living picture! We've never presented you with that before, and it might make all the difference!"

And laughing at the utter confusion on Mark's face, Charlotte walked to a door on the other side of the room. To Mark's astonishment, a lovely young woman came in. She had hair that was a shiny burnished brown, hanging down her back in a braid which went down past her hips. Her face was a tiny oval in shape, with lovely warm brown eyes. And, thought Mark-she looks intelligent as well as lovely.

Charlotte saw the effect the girl had on him. She put him out of his misery. "This is Miss Maud Penhurst. She is actually a very distant relation. Do you remember the Albright branch of the family? Well, many years ago, an Albright female married a Penhurst. They are her direct ancestors." She looked at Sarah. Neither of them believed Mark had heard a word.

"Maud, dear, have a seat." Sarah got the girl to sit. Then she signaled Mark to come with her and Charlotte. "Now listen. Maud is not some peasant girl to have a swing with. If you wish to be with her, you must marry her. Do you understand? I have told her everything about you-yes, everything," she said. "As I said, she is no peasant, and she must know about you before she makes the decision to marry you. I've told her what a challenging time you have settling to one woman. Whether that will be alright, or sit hard with her, only she knows, and only she can decide. Your line must continue, Mark. Treat her well."

Then, leaving the young man and young woman to talk privately, the two women went back into the drawing room, feeling they had done their duty.

36

The Laurels (1667)

Thomas Mowbray sat in the common room of his manor house, smoking his pipe.

"What do you guess there'll be a wedding soon? I saw Sarah and Charlotte with Mark. Josh told me, too. There's a young woman staying with Sarah, and they hooked her up with him. Don't know too much about her, but I caught a glimpse of her in the hall-pretty young thing. I think he'll do it-after all, he can have his fun on the side, so long as he fills the nurseries." Living all these years with Anne had made him more vulgar than he used to be.

He knew the family had never forgiven him for putting Natalie aside for Anne. To choose between them was like chalk and cheese! But he had done only what they wanted Mark to do-keep his line from dying out.

He married a very heavily pregnant Anne Milligan less than a month after Natalie had been set aside. To Thomas' satisfaction, they now had three children: nine-year-old Gabriel, eight year-old Daniel, and seven-year old Sophia. Anne had certainly proven her fertility, but the family felt she was not Carrington-Grey material, and though they showed her civility, it was blended with a shade of coolness in their cultured, well-bred tones.

Thomas, after ten years with his second wife, found himself occasionally missing Natalie. Natalie, with her calm, smooth demeanor, was very different from crass, common, Anne, who yelled and shouted more than she spoke softly. However, it was

Anne who had given him children, while Natalie had not, or could not, so that was that.

Not for the first time, Thomas realized he had married Anne strictly for her proven fecundity. Being the daughter of an innkeeper, she certainly had no highborn connections, and as for looks, her stringy brown hair and colourless grey eyes left a great deal to be desired. She was uneducated and crass. Definitely not someone who should marry into high society. Thomas knew he would have been forgiven if he had replaced Natalie with someone of her own rank. Well, the woman had given him three children. As the years progressed, and her looks, never very good to begin with, receded, he found fulfillment of his own needs with pretty prostitutes in the village.

Looking at Anne now, he said, "On the thought that there may be a wedding, I'll give you a bit extra, so's you can buy yourself some material for a gown, and some falderals."

Anne replied, "I'll take the money, and gladly, husband. But it's a waste. I'll save it for the house."

She jumped as Thomas banged his fist on the table. "Anne! You are not my housekeeper-you are my wife! We have servants. Will you, for once, stop thinking like an innkeeper's daughter, and think like the wife of a nobly-born squire? You will get new things. You will not put me to shame. If there's a wedding, I want you to be prepared. It'll take you longer than most, so get started quickly," he added cruelly. But sarcasm was wasted on Anne. She nodded, and left the room.

Thomas closed his eyes. It wasn't Anne's fault-he found himself snapping at her more and more. It was his fault. He missed the quiet conversations with his first wife. But if I stayed with her, it would have been a childless state. Everything in life must be bought and paid for, he thought. How true that was, especially in his case.

Anne Mowbray sat in the solar, quietly doing some plain sewing. Embroidery had never sat well with her-she had never learned. In her world, why sew if you didn't need to? When sheets and clothing needed repair, then you sewed them. She had no time for ladies doing pretty sewing.

She looked up from her work, and gazed out the window. The view showed her the turrets of Colbert Castle.

She would never forget the day Thomas brought her to Colbert ten years ago. Anthony's father was the earl then. She had sat in the drawing room of the old castle, very heavily pregnant, and looking around her with awe, while the earl, smiling a frozen smile at her, had said, "Thomas, may we speak?" Then the two had left the room. She could hear their mutterings, with snatches of words. "...innkeeper!" "...not for us."

Well, they had married, and she, with her large belly, had to be accepted. She had made no move to try to be like the other women of the family-it just wasn't in her to do so. She was a simple peasant woman, from peasant stock, and now, she was elevated to being a part of a large family network, that lived in beautiful castles, like Colbert, some of them were dukes, some, earls. She couldn't believe her luck.

She had simply been helping her father serve in the inn, when Master Thomas Mowbray had come in. After serving him the ale he ordered, he had looked her up and down, drank his drink, and left. The next day, he spoke to her. The day after that, he offered to take her on a little excursion down the river. Her father, she noticed, had shown no objection. He knew very well who Master Mowbray was, and it was in his best interest for his daughter to be involved with such a man.

On the little excursion, Anne conceived. She was not in love with Thomas. She saw him as a step up out of the life she had. And Thomas, she knew, was only using her as a breeding cow. He had told her, quite plainly, that he had a wife, but was going to set her aside, and put her in her place, if she conceived. So, there was really equality on both sides. Now, after ten years, she saw the wistful glances he sometimes gave. There was nothing he could do about it now. She was his wife, the mother of his children, and Lady Natalie was not. She wasn't jealous. She had what she wanted: a good home and a good name, and children. She was content.

37

Ainsleigh Hall (1668)

LADY Charlotte was reading her correspondence in her private office. Suddenly, her eyes opened very wide. "Oh my!" Picking up the missive, she walked out of the room, to her husband's office.

The Duke was busy with his letters as his wife came into the room, saying, "Lucas! You have to hear this!"

"What is it dear? Calm down, and tell me your news."

"Well, this letter is from Natalie-Thomas' first wife. Remember her?"

"Of course, I remember her. What about her? Is she well?"

Charlotte held the letter up. "She's more than well, Lucas. She recently married Trevor, and just had a baby boy!" The person in question was Trevor Gaines, the Duke of Pondshire. His wife had died two years ago. Now, Natalie was his duchess! And she had a baby!

The Duke looked at his wife. "Are you certain?" Taking the letter from his wife, he read through. "Trevor always had a smile for her-I used to think he was secretly in love with her, even when Lucy was alive. Well, good for her-and it serves Thomas right to be stuck with that old drudge."

Charlotte said nothing, but she thought the same thing. "Well, I'm going to write to Sarah. She would love the news."

Lucas looked at his wife. "Lotty, I wonder how this will affect Thomas."

Charlotte replied, "It should affect him not at all. Natalie is now free to make her own choices. And it's been over ten years. What will bother him, I think, is that she had a child. But that was his choice to annul their marriage-if he had been patient, he might have had a child with her-maybe, we'll never know. Now, as you say, he's stuck with Anne."

38

Castle Pondshire (1668)

LADY Natalie Gaines, Duchess of Pondshire, was sitting in a chair in the nursery of the castle. Every now and then, she'd get up, and see her sleeping son, Travis. You are my miracle baby, she thought. I love you so much.

Turning at the sound of footsteps, she smiled as the nurse entered the room. "My lady, the little lord sleeps very well. He's as good as gold. I'll let you know when he wakes."

Natalie took the hint. In certain parts of the household, servants ruled supreme. The kitchens, and the nursery, were both out of bounds for the lord and lady.

Placing a kiss on her sleeping son, the duchess walked out of the room, down the long, winding staircase. She decided she would talk to Trevor about having a very small house party-to show off the baby, she thought, smiling inwardly. And the only people she wanted to invite were the families of Charlotte Gaines and Sarah Treaves. While she was married to Thomas, Charlotte and Sarah were her partners in crime. The three ladies did everything together, and when they met at family functions, all three would join and host.

She smiled to herself. She was smiling a lot these days, she realized. She thought back to when Trevor got down on one knee and declared his undying love for her. Older than him by eight years, Natalie had felt flattered, but did not think it would go further than that. However, Trevor had persisted, and she was now his duchess, and the mother of his only child. His first wife, alas, had died, leaving him childless.

She harboured no ill will towards Thomas. He had gotten his wish, but he was stuck with a woman who could never be a proper companion to him. It must be a very lonely marriage, she thought. Not for the first time, she wondered why Thomas had not married a lady of rank. She and Thomas had always gotten along well with each other. Even when they parted, they had parted amicably, each knowing the reasons, and understanding them. Now, she thought- I'm not barren! It just took me a long time.

Going to her private office, the duchess happily wrote her invitations to her friends.

39

Stafford Castle (1671)

Lady Maud Stafford gazed fondly at her three-year-old son, Sebastian, playing on the thick carpet by her feet, as she did her embroidery. She adored the little boy-he was the image of his handsome father. Her smile faltered.

After four years of marriage, she and Mark got on very well. Mark stayed entranced by his lovely wife, and the two of them had wonderful discussions on the Greeks, theology, and other topics. He also asked for her aide in the running of the estate, which she was happy to give.

But it was just around the middle of this fourth year, she had noticed, that things had started to change. They still talked, Mark still held her at night, but not every night, and some nights, he wasn't home. She had been warned about this-she was married to a man who just couldn't stay committed for long. The fact he had been solely with her for four years, was an amazing feat in itself. Well, she had thought, stoically. I had to know this day would come. Now I must say: Do I resign myself to sharing him, or losing him completely? The answer, to her, was obvious. Of course, she wouldn't lose him. She knew he loved her. But he couldn't stay faithful-it was not in his nature.

He had a long talk about it to her once. "Sweetheart, I am so sorry. You made a bad bargain marrying me. That day, with Charlotte and Sarah, you had the choice, and you made the wrong one. But don't leave. I do love you, Maud, I really do. But what they said, it's true. I can't stay with one. Unfortunately, that'll never change. I leave the choice up to you. But please, know that I love and treasure you-with the others, there is no feeling."

And she had replied, "There is no choice to make. I love you, too, Mark." And they had hugged each other, each one knowing that this would be the beginning of a long heartache.

Mark thought, I knew I wasn't meant for marriage. I have done my duty. I even fell in love with my wife. I love my son. But why can't I stop seeing another? He didn't tell Maud, but there was only one other woman he was seeing: Yolande Laurent, his old paramour. She was the one who had the hold over him. Her voluptuous features were a stark contrast to Maud's slim, elegant figure, and Mark felt he could not, and would not, get enough of it. But he never brought her in the castle-he wouldn't insult Maud by bringing his mistress into his wife's home. Also, he felt that by telling Maud there was more than one, it would lessen their import in her eyes.

In truth, the curvaceous Yolande meant as much to him as his wife did, but in a very different way. He felt no love for her, and hardly affection, too. He just wanted her physically. After a day, maybe two days with her, the old revulsion would appear, and he would leave to go back home to his wife, and he would stay until the old hunger overtook him again. He never wanted his life to change: he felt he had the best of both worlds. But he said to Yolande once, "Never show your face in my castle, never go near Maud. If she ever sees you and suspects who you are, I will have you killed. Do you hear? I will have you killed. I won't have my wife hurt any further."

And Yolande, with a little seductive laugh, trailing her fingers down Mark's bare back, replied, "Never fear, my lord. It shall be as you wish. You will always have your old Yolande, and your lady wife will be home waiting for you. You will have us both-and I will keep away from her. After all, it isn't her I want."

Then, Mark, realized, the disgust was showing up. By morning, he would be feeling awful. Time to go home to Maud. Closing his eyes, he thought, sleepily, it can wait till morning. I'm too tired. I'm sure she won't mind.

40

Ainsleigh Hall (1671)

THOMAS Mowbray was striding the floor of the private office of the Duke. He was highly agitated, Lucas noticed.

"Sit down, man. Here, relax, breathe deeply. Now," as the man visibly calmed down. "I know why you're upset. But it's over with, you know. After all, little Travis is three years old. By God, have you been acting this way for three years? I must say, I was never overly-fond of Anne, but I must say, I pity her now, more than I can say."

Thomas seemed not to hear. "That should have been my baby!"

Lucas looked at him, shocked. "It wasn't meant to be, Tom. Now, look. You had better stop talking like this. If it ever comes to Trevor's ears, he will likely call you out, cousin or no. And you don't want to fight him. He's practically ten years your junior, and he'll definitely beat you. Besides, it's nothing to fight over. You and Natalie parted amicably, now she has a child, and you have your children. You are both fortunate. Obviously, you still have feelings for Natalie-but you are now married to Anne."

Thomas bent his head. Then swallowing deeply, he chose his words with care. "You are right, of course, Lucas. And I have been doing a disservice to Anne. All of these years. Whatever she's like, she is my wife, and she deserves to be treated as such. I'll go home now. Thank you for letting me blow off my steam. Clearly, I couldn't do this at home."

Lucas smiled. "I'm glad I could help. And remember, Thomas. Natalie deserves the same as you-a home and family, and now she has both."

Thomas got on his horse, and directed the animal to walk on the lane towards home. He was in no hurry. The slow walk of his horse, with its rhythmic cadence, gave him an opportunity to think, while calming him further.

Lucas had been correct, of course. He remembered how he felt, when he first found out about Natalie's baby. He didn't remember what he said, but he knew he was shouting it, and it wasn't repeatable. In the three years since, he had treated Anne like a stranger. His children, too, had suffered. Luckily, they had been away from home when the news had come, but after they got home, they saw the coldness of their father toward their mother. As for Anne, she had waited with the patience of a peasant, for her husband to get over this latest news.

Thomas spurred his horse on. Well, it was time for Anne's patience to be rewarded. He must stop acting the part of a jealous fool. Spurring the horse faster, Thomas made for his home,

promising himself he would do all he could to make it up to his wife. But when he thought of his wife, he saw Natalie's beautiful, well-bred face. Replacing that with Anne's course, unattractive one, Thomas swallowed, and thought, I'll make it up to Anne. He knew his irritation with his wife would not stay away for long, and that, as always, it would be his fault. The price I pay, he thought, the price I pay.

41

Stafford Castle (1680)

TWELVE-YEAR-OLD Sebastian Stafford came down from the schoolroom to his father's private office. After all these years, Mark had not changed a great deal, except for a touch of grey hair at his temples.

"I've done my sums, Father, if you would like to see." The young boy rarely smiled. The servants of the castle said he had stopped smiling when his mother died two years ago.

Maud, Lady Stafford, died of the childbed fever after giving birth to a baby daughter. The baby had only lived for two hours after her mother died. So now, in the large castle, with only servants for company, lived the Earl and his twelve-year-old son.

"Well, you've done superb, as usual, Sebastian. I always had difficulty with sums, but they come easily to you." Mark looked at his son, and felt he hadn't done right by this boy of his and Maud's-his heir.

After Maud died, he went into deep mourning, and locked himself up in his rooms. After a month or so, he came out, and he and the boy remained inside, going nowhere else. But eight months after his wife's death, he felt the familiar beckoning of Yolande. At first, he didn't want to leave the child alone in the castle, but as he thought to himself-he is surrounded by servants.

He appointed a special manservant to look after Sebastian, and stay with him in his rooms when he was out with Yolande. And soon, he was back to his old habits again.

Yolande had even hinted to him that now he was a widower, she might come to the castle, as in the old days. He had jumped at that. "Never! My son lives there. You are not to go near him. The same rules apply, Yolande. See that you follow them."

To which, Yolande murmured assent. To herself, she thought, I have heard it said his son is as handsome as he is. I must keep my looks-when he is older, who knows? I could have father, and son!

Sebastian looked at his father. He loved Mark, but he had no illusions about him. He had known, when he was old enough to understand, all about his father's lecherous ways. He felt rage on his mother's behalf, but he knew she had chosen to put up with it. He had overheard many conversations in this house-after that, it was impossible to remain ignorant of the situation.

Mark sighed inwardly. To this child, he was leaving everything he owned. This child was his only heir, his son. But he had become distant-he couldn't reach him anymore. Mark knew the reasons. It wasn't just Maud's dying, it was his lifestyle. Sebastian highly disapproved of it, but even for the love of his son, he could not stop.

He knew he was beyond hope.

"Come here, son," he said, and leaning forward, gave the boy a much-needed hug. For a few moments, father and son were locked in an embrace, each deriving comfort from the other.

42

Colbert Castle (1681)

A NTHONY Carrington-Grey threw back his head, and let out a huge laugh. No one would recognize in this tall, confident, and elegant young man, the scared, skinny little boy of a few years ago. The earldom sat well with Tony, and he was very content personally.

A few years ago, he married Lady Adriana Pomeroy, and they had a daughter, Eva, who was now five years old.

The other occupant of the room, Mark Stafford, smiled indulgently. How happy he was to see Tony looking so well!

Looking at his favourite cousin, Tony said, "But really, Mark, it is good to see you! Is all well with Sebastian? You should have brought him along, too. How are the two of you getting on?"

"Ah, well, you know thirteen-year-olds," Mark smiled. "I'll bring him next time, I promise. I didn't want his studies interrupted. My word, that boy of mine is a walking brain! He must have inherited it from Maud-definitely not me."

Tony smiled faintly. "Is all well, Mark? You can talk to me, you know that. I know you're still seeing that woman, what's her name?"

"Yes, Tony, I'm still seeing that woman, what's her name, and I'll probably continue until I die, or she does. I've been seeing her since before I got married. It's not likely to end now."

"Ah well, as long as Sebastian doesn't-"

"Sebastian is not involved." This, from the Earl, was sharp-speaking to his favourite cousin.

Raising his hands, Anthony said, "I'm sorry. I didn't mean to pry."

"Thank you," and Tony was rewarded with a big smile.

Before the two could continue, there was a noise at the door. It was opened by a child, the most enchanting child Mark had ever seen. "Uncle Mark!" And little Eva Carrington-Grey bounded into his arms, and was rewarded with a huge throw into the air. Laughing uncontrollably, she shouted, "More!"

Her mother walked into the room. "Now Eva," it is time for bed. Kiss your father and uncle good night, and go with the maid."

"Please father, may I stay?" Bouncing her golden curls, Eva hugged her father.

"Do as your mother tells you, pet." Kissing his daughter good night, he let her walk to Uncle Mark. "Good night, love. Next time, I'll bring Sebastian." He had not sat well in the child's favour for not bringing her beloved cousin along. The maid came and took the girl away.

"What an enchanting child she is!" Mark smiled.

"Yes, and what a little hoyden, too! She certainly knows how to wrap her father around her little finger," laughed the Countess. Anthony had the grace to look guilty.

"Well, gentlemen, I shall leave you, too. I have some letters to write before I retire for the evening." Kissing Mark and her husband good night, Adriana left the room also.

"I'm glad to see you so happy, Anthony. It's been a long ride for you since your early days as earl, but you're sitting on top of things. You've got a lovely wife, and beautiful child."

"Yes, I just need that heir," replied the younger man.

"It'll come in time, God willing," said Mark. "I suppose I'm resorting to gossip, but how are things with Thomas? My estate is further away, I hardly see them, but Tom lives fairly close to Colbert. How is he doing, and that wife of his?"

Anthony sat down. Yes, they were getting down to gossip! "Well, I believe he's alright-now, that is. When he first heard about it, he was awful-I felt for his whole family, especially poor Anne. But she took everything in stride. She's a solid, dependable woman.

"And Sophia is finally married, as you know. It was a good day's work she did when she met that clergyman."

Thomas Mowbray's only daughter inherited her mother's looks, and her father found it very hard to marry her off. She had resigned herself to walking around the village, dispensing religious tracts. Coming across the Reverend Wilfrid Miller in her travels, the two reached their own agreement, and decided to marry. Neither Thomas nor Anne raised any objections. Thomas, in fact, was relieved. He thought he would never get Sophia married off-her homely looks had sent would-be suitors running in the past. Now, she was set for life.

Thomas' older son, Gabriel, married a woman his father chose for him. Thomas was determined for his son not to make the same mistake his father made, so he chose for Gabriel a lovely noble-woman named Theresa Rice.

His middle child, Daniel, decided he wanted to be a sailor, and ran off to join the high seas two years ago. He had not been heard from since.

The two men discussed these and other family matters. "So, all is well with Thomas?" Mark asked again.

"It would seem so. I haven't heard anything different. He's finally accepted Natalie's situation. I heard tell he even mentioned to Josh that he could finally be happy for her. So, I suppose all is well with him."

"Ah, well, then that is to the good." Rising up from his chair, Mark said, "And now, little cousin, I'll away to my bed. I must leave early tomorrow morning to be home before dark. Good night."

After his cousin had left the room, Anthony thought, it's you, dear cousin Mark, who is not well. I can see your torment. When

Maud was alive, you had two worlds that you love-of all the women, she was the only one you cared for. Now that she is gone, you're left with nothing, no companion, no helpmeet. And gallivanting with your mistress leaves you emptier, instead of filling you up. How much more can you take?

And shaking his thoughts, the young Earl of Easterbrook went up to his Countess, thinking for the countless time, I don't know what I'd do without my Adriana. I need an heir, we must try for another child, but I don't want her to suffer the dangers of childbirth, like Maud. He knew there was nothing he could do. It was the will of God whether woman died or survived-but he knew he would be just as lost without Adriana as Mark was without Maud.

43

Castle Colbert (1682)

Anthony bent down to wipe his wife's brow. "Are you all right, my love?" He was so worried about Adriana, he scarcely had taken in that he now had a son and heir.

The countess lay back on the pillows, her face pale. "Yes, dear. I may not look well, but I know I will fully recover. Don't worry so much." She reached out to stroke his face. Childbirth had always been difficult for her-more than for most, and Anthony was terrified he would lose her.

At that moment, the midwife came in with a little bundle. "And, my lord, you have a son-here is the little lord!" And she put the bundle into his arms.

Anthony stepped back. "He's too small. I don't want to drop him." "You won't," laughed the Countess. "Now give me my son-I wish to see him." The sleeping child was put in his mother's arms.

Adriana's mother, Annette, was also in the room. "You're not going to give him that peculiar name, are you?"

"Cayden is not a peculiar name -it's unusual and unique. It will be appreciated. Besides, he's our's, and we'll name him what we wish."

Anthony's snub kept the older woman quiet. Really, thought the Earl-she presumes too much.

"Adriana, you must think about having another. One heir is not enough."

Anthony had enough. "Annette, your daughter has just recovered from a heavy labour. I think she needs her rest now, don't you think?" And guiding the woman outside, he said, "I will thank you not to say things that will upset my wife. If you can't control your speech, your visit will be cut short."

Annette gazed long and hard at her son-in-law. He truly loved her daughter. Suddenly, she smiled. "Very well, Anthony. I can see your concern is only for her. That tells so well in your favour." And to Anthony's surprise, the woman gave him a kiss on the cheek, then turned and walked away. I won! He smiled, and walked back into his wife's room.

44

Stafford Castle (1685)

SEVENTEEN-YEAR-OLD Sebastian Stafford got his horse from the stables, and set off on down towards the village. Once in awhile, he liked to go to the tavern, have a drink, and talk to John Perry, the tavern owner.

Mark, at forty-seven, did not go out as often as he used to. He was still a very good-looking man, but he found there was now more enjoyment to be had in the comfort of his home. He would often sit and read in the library during the evenings after the dinner hour. Also, Anthony threw a large party when his son was born, and at that party, Mark met a woman. It was strange for him-there was no physical aspect about his relationship with her, but he felt something deeper. They met often, to take rides in the countryside, and have dinner together. They would discuss topics. His relationship with Mrs. Trefusis was, Mark realized, the most satisfactory one he had ever had with a woman. Even his relationship with his wife had not been as good. As a result, his mistress, Yolande, had some moments of deep suffering.

However, as always, she was very good at going to her alternate plan. Years ago, she had planned to seduce Mark's son, if he was good-looking enough.

One day, while Sebastian was in the village tavern, Yolande, who had awaited her moment, sidled up to him.

She had kept her figure, and by what artificial means, only she knew, had kept her hair as black as it was when she was very young. Her skin was still as soft and supple as ever, and her still curvaceous figure remained taut and smooth. When she accosted the Earl's son, Sebastian saw a beautiful, black-haired woman, with a sultry look and a gorgeous figure.

Yolande, in her turn, saw a young man that was not only the image of his father when younger, but even more handsome. Immediately, she thought, I must have him!

And Sebastian thought, as he linked his arm through her's, I'll have a beauty tonight! He had no idea who she was. To him, she was quite young. She didn't look his father's age.

As they were leaving, the tavern owner, said, "My lord, a moment!"

"What is it, my good man?" Sebastian comes to the man.

"Please, my lord, may I speak to you here, in my inner room?"

Excusing himself, Sebastian followed the man inside the tiny room. "What is it, John? I'm anxious to be off, and you can see why!"

"Oh, my young lord, don't you know who that woman is?"

"Who is she?" Replied Sebastian, but for some reason, he felt his insides clench.

"My dear young lord, she's your father's former mistress, begging your pardon, sir. She has been with him since before your father married. We all know your father has slowed down his visits to her, or has stopped seeing her altogether, and that's why she's hooked onto you. She's a bad woman, my lord. You mustn't see her."

"Mustn't? You can't tell me who I should see and who I shouldn't."

"Oh, my lord, I say this as a friend. She is no good. And for you to be with a woman that your father--well, sir, you must realize, it's indecent. The Earl wouldn't approve."

"What my father approves of or doesn't approve of simply does not concern me anymore, John. He's the last person to give his approval or disapproval for anything. I love him, don't get me wrong, I truly love him. But as for any respect-I lost all respect for him in my early childhood-when I was old enough to know about his lifestyle. So, you see, he would be the last one to judge me."

John rubbed his forehead in agitation. He really liked the Earl's son. "But don't you see, Sebastian? You're only repeating your father's behaviour. The very behaviour you said you don't respect."

Sebastian put a hand on his friend's shoulder. "Thanks for caring, my friend. But don't worry. Yolande is the most amazing-looking woman I've ever met. I must have her-even though she was once my father's. You must admit, she's aged well! So, I'll have my fun with her for awhile. But I will end it-very soon. She won't hold a spell over me like she did with my father."

So saying, the young man turned and left the room. John saw the Earl's son hold the paramour around the waist, as they left the tavern.

Yes, he thought, she's aged well-the Earl will be livid if he learns she's been near his son. Didn't he once threaten to have her killed if she did? Well, the boy is practically an adult now, thought the tavern keeper. There's not much the Earl can do. He should let this relationship run its course. Sebastian was not like his father-he was made of finer stuff. He wanted Yolande because of her exotic looks, but she was really not his type; he would tire of her, and drop her soon. If the Earl took action, the young man would never forgive him, and would adopt a course that would make his father very sorry indeed.

But it's not my place, thought John. I'm Sebastian's friend-not his father's. Hopefully, he'll be smart about this-if only for his son's sake.

45

Stafford Castle (1686)

MARK Stafford paced the floor of his private office, his hands behind his back. He couldn't believe what he heard! Just wait, he thought. He had given very firm instructions to the servants to inform Sebastian his father wanted to speak to him the moment he returned.

A few minutes later, Sebastian, himself, walked into the room, and to the Earl, his son was acting jaunty as ever. He actually wanted to hit the boy for his foolishness.

"We will talk, and now," the Earl's voice was calm, and deadly.

"What about, Father?" Sebastian fell into a chair, casually swinging his legs over the arm.

"You will answer me truthfully, Sebastian, and you will answer me now. Have you been seeing the paramour, Yolande Laurent?"

"I'm eighteen, now, and not likely to be a virgin. Surely someone like you must know that."

"That's not what I asked you," Mark's temperature rose. "I asked about her specifically."

"And what if I have? To answer you, yes, for a year now. But I got tired of her and broke it off six weeks ago. Are you jealous, Father? If so, are you jealous that I had your mistress, or are you jealous that I was able to cut her off, whereas she controlled and held you, body and soul, for years?"

Mark lunged forward, and in a split second, felt his own fist make contact with his beloved son's face.

"Sebastian! I'm so sorry!" Trying to help his son up, Mark felt like a further useless parent when the young man shoved his father aside, got himself up, and walked towards the door.

With one handle on the doorknob, Sebastian turned to his father, about to say something. Then, changing his mind, the younger man left the room, leaving his father standing in the middle of it. "Oh Maud, what have I done? My actions of years ago are affecting our boy in a way I never dreamed of. What shall I do, my dear? How can I make this right?" And he thought he heard his wife's voice in the distance saying, "You can't. It's too late."

The Earl remained standing in the middle of the room, tears streaming down his face, until his manservant came and called him for dinner.

46

Stafford Castle (1713)

SEBASTIAN, Lord Stafford, paced around his desk. He had experienced tremendous feelings of guilt when his father died nine years ago-he didn't feel bereavement in any way. He had always loved Mark-but in the last few years, his love for his father had slowly ebbed the same way his respect had, years before. Therefore, when Mark died, his son succeeded to his title on nothing more than a sombre note.

Now, at the age of forty-five, Sebastian felt he had come a long way from the young boy who swived his father's mistress. Shaking his head, the Earl thought of the follies of youth.

Thinking about the terrible interview with his son last night, he thought about his pride and joy-his only lawfully-begotten child and heir, Simon. They had argued, no, fought, over Simon's refused marriage proposals. At twenty-three years of age, Simon very much resembled his handsome grandfather, Mark. It appeared that Simon, the future Earl, was not interested in marriage at all. He had vehemently turned down any offers that were put before him, sending prospective fathers-in-law away politely, but firmly. Sebastian had raged. Alicia had cried. This could not be! He is nothing like me, Sebastian thought-and everything like my father-oh, how angry that makes me! For all his life, Sebastian had very little love, and absolutely no respect, for his father, and his lifestyle.

Having spoken to his wife long into the night, Sebastian prepared for his interview with his son. They had reached a decision, and it must be abided by.

The personable young man walked into the room warily. "Good morning, Father."

Sebastian recalled another interview in this office between father and son, only he had been the son then. And I was a cheeky bastard, too, he thought. Simon was nothing like him. He was charming, yes, and very mannerly, too. He got that from his mother-heaven knew the Staffords were mannerly only if they got their own way.

"Good morning. I have made my decision. Truly, I don't understand your strange disinclination for marriage. You seem to be a great deal like my father-your grandfather, Mark Stafford. The two of us were not close. He, too, it is said, had a great dislike of the married state. But, all of that is neither here nor there.

"As the heir, you *have* to marry and have children. On the side, you can have as many lovers as you wish. Only be discreet, I don't wish to tarnish the Stafford name. As to whether you tell your future wife, that is up to you."

Simon leaned forward. "You don't want to tarnish the family name? Father? Is that *you* talking? With Grandfather Mark's background, not to mention your little peccadillo-how old is he now-eighteen, I believe? At least Mark was smart not to leave any little consequences behind. What part of our name isn't tarnished already?"

"That will do, Simon. Now, a bride for you has already been chosen-you're twenty-three already, so there's no time to waste. Most of the men of our family have been married by eighteen or nineteen at the latest. Your mother and I were lenient with you-no more. Her name is Marlene McBride, and she's a lovely young woman, a well-connected-daughter of a friend of your mother's family. The wedding, by the way, is in three weeks' time. Your mother and I expect a grandchild next year-after that, do whatever, with whomever, you wish, provided you fill the nursery every year or two."

Then, the Earl got up and left the room, leaving his son staring after him, a mask of naked hatred on his face.

47

Feeney Cottage (1713)

SEBASTIAN was just about to knock on the door, when it was opened by a diminutive woman. Andrea Feeney, at thirty-six years of age, was still lovely to look at. Her deep brown hair was soft, smooth and shiny. She had it tied back in a bun. Her eyes were a soft brown, looking like the eyes of a roe deer. Sebastian never got tired of looking at her. Every time he came here, the words, 'Like father, like son,' played in his head. But I'm not like him. I'm not. Somewhere in the distant corners of his mind, he could swear he heard the tinkling laugh of the long-dead Yolande.

He held up his latest offering-a fat capon. "We went on a hunting party, and I saved one for you." Reaching down, he placed the bird on the table, then he held the woman by the waist, and gave her a gentle kiss on the lips. That was all it would be. Since the birth of John, eighteen years ago, all sexual commerce between them had ceased, at Sebastian's behest. He just couldn't-he felt the overwhelming guilt was going to eat him alive.

He was already married to Alicia when he met Andrea. Simon was only four years old when Andrea became pregnant with John. And Alicia found out about his mistress. There followed a time of guilt, sadness, anger. It made Sebastian wonder how on earth could his father handle such a lifestyle so contentedly, and not be torn apart by those emotions. That's why he knew he was different.

So, after John's birth, he had stayed away for awhile. Until one day, Alicia came to him and said, "You have another son. He deserves a father as much as Simon does."

The woman was a saint. As he kissed her, and made ready to go, Alicia held his sleeve. "You have two sons, now, Sebastian, but you still have only one wife. Please, if all else fails you, please remember that."

And because of Alicia's ready acquiescence of his bastard child, he owed it to her to break off all physical ties to the baby's mother.

Andrea had a very sweet disposition, and after hearing of the Countess' acceptance, had readily agreed. Since then, the Earl would visit his other son and his mother, but would never stay. Instead, he liked to talk to Andrea about topics of interest-how his family was.

Today, after sitting down and receiving a mug of warmed ale, he asked, "Where's John?"

"Would you believe, he met a young woman in the village. Oh my, I can't believe he's grown up. "

"You should have married, Andrea."

Andrea looked at him. "Where is this coming from?"

Sebastian looked down at his ale. Choosing his words carefully, he said, "You know there will never be anything between us again. You've spent eighteen years here, and for what? A few moments of bliss, and the joy of our son. But that son is grown. And you have no husband to keep you company in later years. I can't come here a great deal, you know that. You're still quite young, and attractive."

"Thank you. And I know you can't come here a great deal. Any time you can is nice, but don't think my time is empty. Even without John, there is a lot here to keep me happy and occupied. I do not want marriage. Even if you were free, and I was of noble birth, I wouldn't marry you-marriage was never my choice of a happy life. I am content the way I am." And with that, she picked up his empty ale mug, and took it to the kitchen.

At that moment, the door was flung open, and it looked like Mark Stafford had come to life! Young John Feeney was the very image of his grandfather, the old earl. Sebastian thought, put John and Simon side by side, and they could be twins.

"Why Father! Hello!" Bending down, the young man gave the older a squeeze.

"Be careful, boy, you'll break some of these old bones!" Sebastian laughed. He felt such a sense of pride whenever he saw John. And not for the first time, he thought, if only. For, not only had Alicia been accepting of John, she had allowed him into the castle to have his education with his half brother, Simon. As a result, the young man was graceful, well-bred, and well-educated. With his looks and connections, he was good future husband material for anyone. And, thought Sebastian wryly, he is eager to settle down and marry, unlike Simon.

Kissing his mother, the young man said, "I must leave again, Mother. I'll be home for dinner."

"Wait! Where are you going now?"

"I'm seeing Susan home. I'll see you. Good-bye, Father." And the boy was gone, as quickly as he had come.

Sebastian threw back his head and laughed at Andrea's bewilderment. "He's a lad, Andrea. That's what lads do.

"I was thinking," he said. "It's a pity that John isn't the one born on the right side of the blanket. Now, Simon must marry and couple with a wife to make babies-something he does not want to do. He's too much like old Mark. To John, however, that would be the most wonderful thing, because even as a young child, he has wanted to get married and have a family."

"That is the way of it, poor Simon. But mark my words, Sebastian, and mark them well. No matter what happens. The earldom goes to Simon and his children. If Simon has no children, it should go to someone else in the family-there are enough noble Carrington-Grays, Gaines, or Treaves to pick from. I'm not ambitious for my John to steal it-and I have raised him that way-to never expect it. Lady Alicia has been very good to us, and I will return the favour by not stepping above my place."

"I know. We have discussed this before. I will gift John with a parcel of land, and a little manor house. Then, I will find a nice young lady for him-after all, she will be my daughter-in-law, she will be of good birth. Unless, of course, John beats me and chooses for himself!"

And laughing, the Earl said good-night, and rode his horse down the mile-long road back to the Castle.

48

Haversleigh Hall (1732)

JOHN Feeney, or Haversleigh, as he now went by, looked very young for his thirty-seven years. Looking around him, he had every reason to be completely happy, but he was not. For no one, he knew, could be completely happy-there was always something. And he was no exception.

He had many blessings. He thought of Julia, his wife. Julia was a young woman his father picked for him. Old Sebastian Stafford was determined his beloved bastard son should have as high born a lady as was possible, given his birth. He had been educated at the castle with his half-brother, he had all the rudiments of nobility-except his father was not married to his mother. Even so, his father was able to secure his marriage to the daughter of a rich knight. As her dowry, she brought the beautiful manor house, Haversleigh Hall.

Very shortly after his marriage, he changed his surname, on the advice of his wife. She very quickly pointed out that it was ridiculous for a man named Feeney to be master of a house named Haversleigh. To John, who wanted to please everyone, especially his wife, this made a lot of sense, so he fell in with her wishes. Since his mother was now long dead, her feelings wouldn't be hurt. And his children would be born bearing the more noble surname. 'Feeney' wouldn't have gotten them far, John said to himself.

Leaning back still further in his chair, John reminisced even more. He thought back to the time when Jordan was born. The extreme feeling of joy that pulsated out of him! He couldn't believe he was a father. Then, four years after Jordan, came little Julia.

All is complete, John thought. I have a wonderful wife, beautiful children, a beautiful home-I should be completely happy-but I'm not, and of course, I know the reason—Simon.

John worried incessantly about his half-brother. For Simon and his wife, Marlene, had never had any children, and it seemed they never were going to.

John was the only person in their whole world, to whom Simon had told the real reason behind his, Simon's, reluctance to marry. Simon had confided to John he found the whole business of intimacy with a woman replusive, however, he had continued to do so, but after nineteen years of marriage, the Earl and the Countess were still childless. John was still sitting, thinking about Simon, when a servant came to him. "Sir, a message for you, from the Earl."

Taking the message, John read it. He had just finished reading, and stood up, when his wife entered the room.

The Honourable Julia Haversleigh was very much in love with her husband. When it was put to her that she would be marrying the bastard son of the Earl of Stafford, she had protested-she was made of better stuff than to be thrown away on an illegitimate child!

Then, when she met the young man who was to be her husband, she changed her mind very quickly. He was very handsome, and extremely well-bred and well-educated. One would not take him for a child born 'on the wrong side of the blanket.' In addition, she had thought: he may be a bastard son, but he was the bastard son of an Earl. There may be some rewards coming her way in the future. There was just that common surname of his-'Feeney.' She could not go through her life with such a common appellation. So, being a spoiled only child, she persuaded her father to give her Haversleigh Hall, the second family home, as a dowry. Her plan was to have her husband change his name to 'Haversleigh' so she wouldn't have to have 'Feeney' as a married name. And her father, who could refuse her nothing, was happy to oblige his beloved daughter.

Sebastian, who was going to give John a manor house of his own, was quite pleased he didn't have to do so.

And now, after nineteen years of marriage and two children later, she found she was still passionately in love with him. But she knew, as much as he loved her, there was an aspect of her personality, the snob aspect, that kept John from showing her the same passion.

Seeing the letter her husband held, Julia saw the Stafford Family Crest. "Is all well, husband?"

"Yes, everything is fine. Simon just wants me over for a chat. Don't wait up, dear. I might be late. Sometimes, my brother and I forget the time as we gossip!"

49

Stafford Castle (1732)

If a stranger had walked into the drawing room of Stafford Castle, he would have been forgiven for thinking he was experiencing double vision. The two men sitting in the room looked as identical as can be, but they were only half-brothers. Both men bore a startling resemblance to their common grandfather, the notorious Mark Stafford.

Simon Stafford, the Earl of Stafford, was the legitimate son of Sebastian, Mark's son. Sitting across from Simon was John Haversleigh, Sebastian's son by his mistress, Andrea Feeney.

Simon and John had always gotten along very well-more like brothers than half-brothers. This was mostly due to the Lady Alicia-Simon's mother. She was the one who had asked for John to be brought into the Castle, and be educated alongside his half-brother. The neighbouring village still spoke of the saintly Countess Alicia.

"What's wrong with you, Simon? You still haven't said. I've been sitting here well over an hour now-Marlene came, sat, and went to bed. It's not like you to be beating around the bush. Just come out and say what you want. It's me, remember?"

Simon stood up, poured a drink from a decanter, which John assumed was for himself. Surprisingly, Simon gave it to him.

"You're going to need this, I think, little brother."

"For heaven's sake, Simon! What is it? You're not dying, are you? Oh God!"

The Earl smiled faintly. "Ever the dramatist, aren't you, John? No, I'm perfectly healthy. There are other, more serious issues I need to discuss with you.

"As you know, Marlene and I have no children. We won't have, ever. Our father did me the greatest disservice by forcing me to marry her. It's made her life hell, too."

John cleared his throat. "Well, Simon, as to that, Marlene was told the full story before you married. It was her choice. Our father even gave her the option to back out-but she chose not to."

"She was young, then, Johnny. She had no idea what a life of emptiness it would be for her. All she saw was the shining coronet of a Countess; the rest, she felt, would not matter. How much it matters, she would find out later. Blast our father!"

"Oh, come, Simon. You know he did the best he could. The best for you that would also be the best for the earldom. If you didn't marry Marlene, it would have been someone else.

"And you're only forty-two. It's still not too late. You and Marlene can still have a baby. I'll keep praying for the both of you."

Simon bent down and put his head in his hands. "No, little innocent brother of mine. You don't understand. It's too, too late. Now, you have always known of my lifestyle. I couple for awhile with Marlene in the attempts at procreation, then, I go out to my lovers. Oh, don't blush, John. It's open knowledge between us. You're the only one I have ever told, but after the first time I mentioned it to you, we never brought it up again. But you know that these lovers of mine aren't women. Let us leave it at that.

"And isn't that humorous? Our father was forever saying how much like Grandfather Mark I am-forever the chaser of women? My God! I believe both Father and Grandfather are spinning in their graves!

"Anyway, it's always been that way. After my little dalliances, if Marlene hasn't quickened, I stay with her a few times more, then I'm on my way again. It's been this way for nigh on twenty years now.

"But something has changed. Last month, I met someone special. There was something so alluring and lovely about him." The Earl sat on the edge of his chair. "John, I'm trying to tell you, that after forty-two years, I've finally fallen in love! I'm in a high state of euphoria, even now, as I'm speaking to you. I can't believe it myself. Everything in the world is brighter, birds are chirping, just for us. Isn't it silly? Me, Simon, a middle-aged man, talking and giggling like a girl of sixteen? But it's true, I tell you! I had to mention this-I couldn't hold it in any longer."

Then, more soberly, the Earl continued. "And that's what brings me to why we are really here. I've told Marlene-I had to. I owe the poor woman that much. Because, you see, now that I've met the person of my dreams, I won't be having physical relations with Marlene anymore."

John jumped up, then sat down. His half-brother's homosexuality had been a painful subject for John to contemplate, or even to discuss. However, it said something for the deep love between the two half-brothers that they could converse about it, and so openly. Therefore, John had no qualms about what he was going to say next.

Choosing his words very carefully, John said, "Think, Simon, just think what you are saying." Then, seeing the Earl was about to speak, he held his hand up and said, "Let me finish.

"Think back to the generation before us-namely-our father. He married your mother. Then, one day, he met my mother, and had an affair with her, resulting in me. But our father never left your mother. No matter what. You are-just what are you proposing to do-is Marlene going to leave the Castle-will-will-he-be moving in?"

"NO. Of course not, silly. Marlene is, and always will be, the Countess of Stafford, till the end of her life. And no, he will not come here-that would be insulting Marlene, and I would never do that. No, but you must realize, that if you fall in love with someone, to have relations with someone else, is cheating on that someone you love."

John snorted. "Well, you have been cheating on your wife since you married her. And now, with this fellow you love-well, the others might be overlooked, but when you put love into it, that would be beyond heartbreaking for Marlene."

"I can't help it!" At that moment, the Earl sounded like a petulant little boy.

John stood up and hugged his half-brother. Simon had led such a difficult life. Because of his inheritance, and his proclivities, his life had been cut in two-trying to do what was expected of him, while not breaking down. I couldn't do it, thought John.

The Earl continued. "I will keep things as they are. Marlene knows-she has to. Each month, I will go spend a week with him. Twelve weeks a year with my beloved is not too much to ask for, is it? Marlene and I will live as friends-we could be really good friends, you know-the pressure to create a child was always hard on us both-at times I hated her, she hated me. Now, we won't have that. It's almost a blessing."

"Well, that's good to think of, that way. But there is one thing you're overlooking: the earldom. If you're not having children, then who is to inherit?"

Simon stroked his jaw. He had to enter into this slowly-he knew John's feelings.

"Well, as to that. Um, Jordan is how old, eighteen, I believe?"

"NO! Absolutely not! You know damn well how I feel about this, Simon!"

"Very well, brother, I'll name you as heir, *then* Jordan."

"SIMON!"

"Little brother, what is the problem? This is a good thing, why can't you see? Jordan would be master of Haversleigh Hall and

Earl of Stafford-everything a proud papa could hope for! Why are you against me in this?"

"You know very well why, Simon. My mother. And your mother. My mother raised me to never accept the earldom. She felt it would be a slap on your mother-and she couldn't bear to do that-not after your mother was so good to us. You see, my name may have changed, but I haven't forgotten my Feeney heritage."

Simon leaned back, thinking. While he was very glad his beloved half-brother now had a noble surname, he didn't care for the woman it came from. Julia Haversleigh was, to his mind, a pure snob, and not a very pleasant woman, either. Simon had discovered this at the time of John's marriage, and his negative feelings about his half sister-in-law had only increased with the years.

Looking at John now, he said, "My mother is dead, John. So is your mother. And our father. They're all dead, and the Earldom of Stafford will be dead, too, if you do not accept this. Think how happy Julia will be when she finds out Jordan will be Earl!"

That was his last trump card. If not for himself or his son, surely, John would do it for his wife. But here, Simon got a shock.

"No, that's all the more reason not to. I love Julia, but I'm not blind to her snobbery."

Laughing, Simon got up, and clapped his brother, hard, on the back. "It's settled, John. I'm making Jordan my heir. I've discussed this with Marlene already-she agrees. There is simply no other way. This way, the Stafford Earldom will remain in the hands of a Stafford descendant. Tell Jordan to come here tomorrow-I have to talk to him about a few things. And by the way, tell him it won't be for years-I don't expect to die anytime soon.

"By the way, John. Jordan will be marrying soon, won't he? Make sure her lineage is a good one-after all, she will be Countess. Now, enough! I've arranged a late supper for us. A guest room has also been prepared-see-it's past three in the morning! Let's go eat, little brother. My goodness, John, such a load off my mind-you can't imagine!"

And the two men walked companionably into the small private supper parlour.

50

Haversleigh Hall (1732)

JOHN looked at his wife. The look of joy on her face had an air of
smugness to it he didn't care for.

They were sitting in the drawing room. John had given his wife
a very abridged version of his conversation with Simon. Sitting up
very straight in her chair, Julia said, "Well, I must say, Simon has
come to a very good decision! Obviously, he has thought it out
long and hard. But you know, dear, Jordan is only eighteen. He
should really have made you his heir."

"I don't believe it. You know, Julia, I always knew that, deep
inside of you, there was a woman who was a snob. Don't get me
wrong, I love you-I always have, but I have no illusions about you.
And to answer you, I'm only five years younger than Simon. It
would be no good naming me his heir-I could even die before him."

"Yes, I suppose you're right. Jordan wasn't overly enthusiastic
when you told him, but I talked him around. Besides, he'll think
differently when we're living at the Castle. I've always wanted to
use the Grand Solar at Stafford-our's is so measly by comparison."

"Julia. I believe you do not quite understand. You and I will be
living here at Haversleigh with Julia until she marries. Then, it'll be
just the two of us." He wondered why that depressed him. "Jordan
will be living at Stafford with his wife, and their children, if God
sends them any. Speaking of that, I must go looking into finding
him one. As Simon pointed out, the lady will be a Countess, she

must come from a proper family." So saying, John left the drawing room to go to his private office.

Julia thought, of course I shall live in the castle. My son needs me. And I need to live in a castle! Oh, why couldn't Simon just hand over his title to John? That way, I could be Countess, and Simon could go and do whatever he wanted, and leave all his responsibilities to John, as he should? As for Marlene-she was jealous of the Countess' title. Marlene could go live in Haversleigh Hall, if she likes.

As she sat there, thinking over this fantasy imagining, a slow, lupine smile came to her face. Everything in this family is all wrong! John is the brother with a family-he should have been named by the old Earl to inherit. She forgot for the moment her husband was illegitimate. Or she didn't care. Sighing, she got up. She had been overly excited when John told her his version of his conversation with Simon. I can still control the situation. I'll end up living in the castle-as for John-he can stay here if he wants. And with that, Julia got up and left the room.

51

Henley House (1743)

R HOSLYN Carrington-Grey, now Rhoslyn Albright, stood in the middle of the old great hall of Henley House in despair. Oh, what's to do, she thought.

Looking around her, at her home for the rest of her life, the new Mistress Albright almost wept. The old manor house was in a vast state of disrepair. There had been no male heirs to the Albright name for over 200 years. The family bred nothing but females that married off into different families, thus causing the name to all but die out, until one of these females, on marrying her husband, somehow, no one knew how, persuaded him to adopted her ancestral name of Albright. She was desperate for the family name to return. That woman gave birth to several male children. Finally! The curse seemed to be lifted.

Now, Rhoslyn was married to one of those descendants: Timothy. Timothy Albright was a very pleasant young man. He had never lived at Henley House; no one in his family had. But he had promised himself that when he married, he would take his wife back to his ancestral home, and raise their family there.

"Don't worry, my love. It won't always be like this. I'll have the workmen on it right away. Very soon, it will be back to its former glory."

"But couldn't we have stayed in town while the repairs are taking place?" asked Rhoslyn. She didn't think that was an unreasonable question.

Timothy shook his head. "The house is big enough for us to live in one side while repairs are underway in the other. Then, we switch sides!" With a laugh, he hugged his new wife.

Rhoslyn smiled. She liked her new husband, she did, truly. But she would never forgive her brother, Russel, for having her marry her to him. Russel wanted Albright back into the Carrington-Grey family, and he was willing to sacrifice his sister to do it. Did he realize he sent her to a dump of a house? If he did, he didn't care. She remembered his words to her as she argued with him.

"Rosie, it's not as big a sacrifice as you play out. Tim Albright is a very good man, I'm told. He has a reputation for treating people well. His family is an old established one. Through the centuries, due to their lack of birthing boys, they have panned away from our family. But you can help largely by bringing them back into our fold. Be sensible about this. You know we all must marry for duty."

Easy for him to say: he was married to the woman of his dreams: Margarita Clarke. True, it had been an arranged, contracted marriage like all theirs's were, but in his case, it had blossomed into love-at least on his side. Rhoslyn still wasn't too sure about her sister-in-law. True, the woman was beautiful-to put it plainly, she was stunning, inviting much admiration from everyone. Was her brother blind, when his wife returned the amorous looks other men gave her? Rhoslyn sighed inwardly. Maybe she shouldn't be so hard on Russel. If not now, for he was still newly-wed, then definitely in the foreseeable future, his wife would be a cause of mischief for him. Well, she thought, Timothy is not a male version of Margarita: he is dependable, sweet, charming, and nice. I didn't want to marry and be chatelaine of this place, but it might not be so bad once it's fixed up.

As if reading her mind, her husband said, "Don't worry, Rhoslyn. You won't recognize this place once it's set to rights. It was once so grand-we'll make it grand again-even grander! And it won't take long-you'll see. I'm so glad we are married, my dear. I have such dreams-you can't imagine. All my life, I've wanted to live here, with my wife and children. You can't imagine what it does to a man-losing his sense of self. For 200 years, my family bred only girls-it must be a record! If it weren't for my grandmother, putting her foot down, and insisting on her new husband adopting the Albright name-well-I don't know."

Rhoslyn stirred. "But is a name all that important? I mean, you would still be you, wouldn't you? Just under a different name. I don't understand that. That's what you and my brother Russel have in common: the love of a name."

"You can't imagine because you are a woman. No, don't take offence-I didn't mean it that way. What I meant is, as a woman, you take on the name of your husband-correct? So, you would not understand the feel of losing it. For a man, it is awful. The Albright name was lost for centuries-my grandmother took steps to bring it back. And through our marriage, your brother took steps to bring it back into the Carrington-Grey fold. I understand that completely. I'll be as good a husband as I can. We will be friends, too. We will be each other's helpmeet. I will love you till the end of my days. You will be the mother of my children. And we will be very happy in this house." Then hugging his wife, he said, "Come. Let's look around. You are the chatelaine-the decorations and design shall be your's. Come, my dear. Let's look around and plan."

Rhoslyn was pleased. Timothy was trying so hard. And she was imagining the picture he had painted. It was very pleasant. Suddenly, she felt she was fortunate, after all.

52

Stafford Castle (1743)

Lady Camille Haversleigh, née Bancroft, the Countess of Stafford, was standing in the middle of her Great Hall, twisting her fingers. She felt faint. She always felt faint when her mother-in-law came to visit. She couldn't stand the woman.

Julia Haversleigh, who couldn't care less what her daughter-in-law thought, glided into the Castle as if she, and not Camille, was the Countess.

"Mother. How nice to see you." Jordan, the Earl, walked quickly into the room, to try to diffuse some of the friction in the air. He knew how impossible his mother could be. With each passing year, she seemed to feel even more strongly that she was owed something she never received, and it made life very difficult for those around her. Jordan could only imagine what hell it must be for his father.

Things had changed almost overnight when Marlene died. She died in 1733, the year after Simon had made Jordan his heir. Simon, heartbroken at losing a friend, nevertheless relinquished his title, and went off to live with his male lover, never to be seen or heard from by the family again, except for the occasional letters he wrote to no one but his half-brother, John Haversleigh.

That same year, Jordan was made Earl. He and his heavily-pregnant Camille had been living at Haversleigh Hall, but on Jordan's rise to the Earldom, the couple moved into Stafford Castle, where, very soon after, the new Countess of Stafford gave birth to their son, Roger. Roger was the first baby to be born at the Castle since Simon, forty-three years ago. It was quite a large celebration for all those around.

John adored his grandson. Little Roger was a pudgy baby, and was the darling of the whole castle. He particularly gurgled with joy when his grandfather came to visit. Now, at the age of ten, he was a handsome, precocious boy.

On this fine day, in 1743, John Haversleigh walked ahead of his wife, into the hall. "Camille, my dear, you are looking very well. I hope I do not disturb you. But, I need to see my little Roger!"

Camille smiled. She liked her father-in-law very much, as much as she disliked her mother-in-law. "He's not so little any more, Father! He's ten years old now!"

Sure enough, from around the corner, the sound of running footsteps, followed by a young boy's voice, could be heard.

"Gramps! Oh, Gramps! I've missed you! Can we go fishing? Father doesn't care for it, and I can only go with you!"

John held the boy close to him. Suddenly, he felt, all of the problems of his life, anything horrendous, even his troubles with Julia, were all worth it if it lead to this very precious boy.

Bending down to kiss the dark curls, he replied, "Of course we'll go! Let me have a word or two with your father, then we shall head off."

The boy hugged his grandfather, then, turning, walked over to Julia, and said, "Hello, Grandmother."

"Hello, Roger. Give me a kiss now," and Roger leaned over to kiss the cold, uninviting cheek. Then, with a child's instinct, knowing the adults wanted to talk, Roger headed off upstairs to patiently await his Grandfather, for the promised fishing treat.

John look at Jordan. "How are things, son?"

"Very good, Father. All is going well. The estate is producing as it should."

"I'm going to the Grand Solar." Julia left the room.

"Father, why does she have to come here all the time? She doesn't come for Roger. She comes because she just wants to be in a castle. It's horrible. And it's driving poor Camille to distraction. She tried to be accommodating in the beginning, but Mother just walks over her-ignoring her. I won't have my wife treated like that in her own home, or anywhere, for that matter. Even if it's my own mother who's doing it. This last time must be the final time."

John rubbed his jaw in irritation. "Tell her what you've just told me. Then give her an ultimatum. Make conditions. This is, after all, your's and Camille's home-it isn't her's."

"You're right." Jordan left them to go to the Solar. Camille, who had been silent up till now, looked at John.

"Oh, Father, what do you think she'll do? How will she react?"

"She will ignore it, and just go on as before, but this is where you and Jordan have to be strong. You have to be *very* firm. Lay down the law, as it were-even to the point of denying her entry. Hopefully, she'll get the message."

Jordan stood in the doorway of the solar. The panelling in the beautiful old room was truly lovely. It was rich old wood. Covering the normally bleak cemented castle walls, the lovely panelling gave the room a warm, glowing feeling. His mother was here all the time. I think it's time to rip out the panelling, he thought, wryly. But no, such a thing is not necessary. I'm putting my foot down. And damn the consequences.

"Mother. Please. I must talk to you."

"Yes Jordan, what is it? By the way, I must talk to Camille. She should have had refreshment sent up to me by now. That is not the proper way to run an establishment. Now, what is it, dear?"

"That is exactly it! Firstly, that is the first time you've mentioned Camille by name, and when you did, it was to criticize. Whenever you come here, you act as if you are the Countess. Get it into your head, Mother. You-are-not. Camille is. She is my wife, my countess, and my beloved. And do not tell me you come here for

151

Roger-you don't. Father comes here for Roger. You come here for yourself. And you treat Camille like dirt. And I am well sick of it. In future, when you come, it will be once in two weeks. And you will not come running up here. This is the private solar of the countess-and you are not the countess. Out of her kindness, Camille has let you use it, but I am going to retract that kindness. You have never thanked her, or even addressed her."

"Are you quite finished?"

"No. Actually, I said that you are to visit no more than once in two weeks. Should you decide to increase that, I will give orders not to gain you admittance."

Julia looked at her son. Then her eyes narrowed. This was Camille's doing. Jordan would never have spoken to her this way before. She thought back, to the time when they were first married. John had chosen her as his son's bride. She came from a noble, old family, the Bancrofts. And she was lovely. She remembered how quiet, and soft spoken she was. They had lived with John and Julia for a year before Jordan rose to the earldom. All that time, she hardly spoke. And now, she thought, she has changed. She thinks that just because she's a countess, she can treat me this way. It's all her fault.

Taking a deep breath and standing up, she replied, "Very well. I shall be calling for the coachman to take me home. Tell your father where I'll be. I'm certain he won't appreciate how I've been treated this day."

"It was Father's idea. He saw how you were driving us mad."

Julia, who had been making her way down the stairs, turned back to look at her son on hearing this statement. "All I ever wanted was what I'm entitled to," she whispered. "I'm a Haversleigh, and I was married to a bastard son. I provided an heir for him-I did my duty. Your grandfather should have made him earl, so I could be countess-after all, I provided the heir-Marlene did not."

Jordan looked down at her in shock. He had always known, but when said out loud, the words were more sinister.

"Everything you have is what you've been entitled to," he said, in a voice devoid of emotion. She really drained him. "You know as well as I-Father could never inherit, because of his bastardry. The only reason I was made heir was because of the situation with Simon. None of us really deserve it. It was Simon's choice. You, Mother, deserve to be exactly where you are. I will get my coach-man to drive you home right now."

And with that, the Earl bounded down the stairs. Julia stared after him. Such was life, she thought. After all her scheming and plotting, it amounts to this. My husband and son against me. Well, I do not care. She went downstairs, and awaited the driver. She didn't bother going into the drawing room, where everyone was sitting. She couldn't face them. She was just going to leave. Serve them right, she thought. They'll feel sorry for treating me like this. And, still feeling that she was in the right, and everyone else was wrong, Julia Haversleigh left her son's home. She didn't make visits once every two weeks-she never returned—much to the relief and delight of the Earl and Countess.

53

Ainsleigh Hall (1750)

TWELVE-YEAR-OLD Peter Gaines, the heir to the dukedom of Ainsleigh, sat with his hands covering his ears. Could it really be possible, he thought? How can one live in such a large castle, and still be subjected to hearing your father yelling at your mother like a peasant? He hated his father.

Walter Gaines, the current Duke of Ainsleigh, was a loud, very unpleasant man. Servants stayed out of his way, even family did not like to cross him. His poor countess had no choice. The intimacy of marriage prevented her from gaining distance.

Sitting in her private parlour, the Countess of Ainsleigh rubbed her face. She got up and walked to one of the many mirrors in the room. They were put there by an earlier duke, for his wife. That wife was the Countess Mina. The face that looked back at her looked like the face of an older woman-someone at least ten years older. He did that to me, she thought.

Walking back to her chair, she sat back heavily. Lying back, with her eyes closed, her mind took her back to the past.

Thirteen years ago, when young Madelyn Kensington was sixteen years old, she was informed by her parents that they had found a handsome duke to be her husband. She remembered how excited she had been. She was going to be a Duchess! Then her father explained about the family, and the duke was a descendant of the famous and beautiful countess, Mina Carrington-Grey. How excited she had been then-the countess Mina was a figure out of history! She was spoken of throughout the county-her beauty was legendary. And now she would be a part of her family of descendants! She remembered her excitement.

Then came the day when she met young Walter Gaines. How handsome he was! Throughout their wedding, she hadn't been able to contain her excitement.

But things had changed. From that moment on, everything went downhill, and had been going downhill ever since.

On their wedding night, he had hurt her terribly. Even now, she shied away from the details. Virgin bride that she was, and therefore ignorant of such matters, she still knew that the things he was doing to her, were terribly unnatural.

The morning after her wedding night, she had put on a robe, and walked out of her bed chamber, leaving her husband sleeping the sleep of the unashamed.

She had walked down the hall, and looked up at the hauntingly beautiful portrait of Walter's famous ancestress, Countess Mina.

Then, she couldn't control herself. Tears started streaming down her face. Looking up at the painting, she whispered, "Why? Why is he like this? Please, my lady, please change him. He is of your blood-he has to be good. I've heard so much about you. Please change him, if you can." The beautiful lady could only smile back at her.

Turning, she had walked into the breakfast parlour, leaving instructions to the maid, that as soon as her husband had left the room, to call her, so she could go get dressed.

This became her habit for ever after. For thirteen years, after a hellish night, she put on her robe, walked to the breakfast parlour, then, after the go ahead from a servant, she went back to her room to dress. Her time was never of her own choosing.

Life had gotten even more difficult after she conceived. But then, all of a sudden, Walter had been told to not touch her because it could harm the baby. So, for nine months, she was given a reprieve, while some maidservant went through the hell she had. Walter had to have some platform on which to work-whether it was his wife or a maid, he didn't care either way.

After Peter was born, Walter started on her again. And he was clever. He saw to it she never conceived again, so she was free to service him.

Madelyn felt she sometimes wanted to kill herself, but her son was the only reason for living-for him, and him alone, she kept going.

Now, as she lay back, thinking of her pitiful, potentially dangerous, marriage, her son came in.

"Mother, why don't you just leave him?"

"Child, he's the Duke. He's not just anyone. I could never leave. I am stuck. The best way to deal with this is just not fight him. Then things don't get so intense."

"I think for you, they've always been intense," Peter muttered.

"That's enough, my dear. Let's not dwell on what we cannot change. Now, why don't you go out for awhile? Get some fresh air."

As Peter bent to kiss his mother, then turn and leave, Madelyn grabbed him, and held him hard. Then, she let him go with a watery smile. "I love you, son. And he loves you, too. And strangely enough, he loves me, too."

"Well, he has a strange way of showing his love for you," and before his mother could react, the boy had left the room.

Yes, thought Madelyn. He has a strange way of showing his love for me. And one day, his 'love' will kill me.

54

Colbert Castle (1750)

L ADY Margarita Carrington-Grey, née Clarke, Countess of Easterbrook, put down her tapestry frame, and got up from her chair. She was bored. And when she was bored, she was, as the servants put it, 'on the prowl.'

No male in the vicinity was safe: she used her dazzling looks to capture him, then, as her sister-in-law, Rhoslyn was fond of saying, she would eat him alive.

Margarita loved her husband. But to flirt with other men was like breathing to her-necessary to life. And she was very careful: no actual sexual activity with her captives: she could not afford a pregnancy outside of her marriage-she was too fond of being a Countess. And she knew that, as much as Russel adored her, he was not willing to share her physically-he would put her aside if she attempted anything with anyone. So, it was an unspoken agreement between them: looking, even touching, and flirting-but none of THAT. And Margarita was happy to comply.

Her husband's family, however, were not so accepting. Rhoslyn, over the years, had grown to positively hate her, calling her a slut and whore in her very presence.

She had overheard an illuminating conversation between brother and sister once.

"Russel, you can't be serious! She's got such a bad reputation now! Put her aside!"

"How can I do that, Rosie? She is the mother to my twins. And not only that, I know the extent she will go to. She won't have physical relations with anyone but me. If she does, she will be put aside. I love her too much to share her favours in that way. As I see it, there is nothing in a kiss or flirtation. Anything beyond that, I can't and won't accept."

"Will you hear yourself? You're going to subject your children to this behaviour, don't you realize? At the moment, Avery and Emma are only five years old, but they will see what their mother is like-it will not please them. And it will set a precedent for Emma-she will grow up thinking a lady may behave that way. Do you really want that for your daughter? And what about yourself? Are you really happy, with your wife kissing and cuddling other men in dark corners of your own castle?"

"Stop it, Rhoslyn. Of course, I don't want that for the children. They will be fine. They're being raised away from their mother's influence-Margarita has never been the maternal type, anyway. She did her duty, and now wants to please herself. Well, and good, so long as she doesn't please herself too much, if you know what I mean.

"As for me, I'm content. I am still having relations with my wife, and I still love her-how could I not? To love someone, you have to accept even their weaknesses. And other men are her weakness. She is abiding by our agreement of not carrying it to the sexual level with them, and for that, I am content-I have to be.

"Now, enough about this topic. Tell me, how is Geoffrey?"

Rhoslyn Albright's face underwent a complete change-from anger, to motherly joy.

"Oh Russel, you can't imagine how clever Geoffrey is! He just turned five, and he knows some of his letters!"

Russel smiled. His sister was such a homebody. She would have been wonderful with six children. Alas, so far, in five years, she and Timothy had been blessed with only one-little Geoffrey, born the same time as Russel's twins. As a result, both parents doted on him. And Geoffrey, born with a sunny disposition, did not spoil with the extra attention, as he otherwise might.

"And why didn't the man of the house come with you on this visit?"

"Oh, Russel, Tim's been very busy-he's just been accepted as head of the Council of Henley Green." Henley Green was the village in the neighbourhood of Henley House. "I'm so proud of him-and he's so excited. He keeps saying that all his childhood dreams are coming true-squire of Henley House, owner of the Albright name, family man. I realized, early on in my marriage, that it doesn't really take a great deal to make Tim a happy man." And with that, Timothy Albright's wife leaned back in her chair, with a contented sigh. Russel saw it didn't take much to make Mrs. Albright a happy woman, either!

"Well," he said. "And to think you were fighting me all the way when I arranged your marriage to him."

"It was the house, Russel. Even before I married Tim, I had heard how dilapidated it had become. That's what I was angry about. Tim, I really liked-it was his family home I hated. Call me a snob, if you like, but after here," she waved her arms around, indicating the Castle, "I just couldn't be mistress of a place like that. But my Tim was as good as his word. He had the place all fixed up, and I had the hand in its decor. And I had plenty of choices to work with-as Tim says-we must spare no expense-it is Geoffrey's legacy, and we mustn't shame him. The Albright name will be back in it's full glory by the time he inherits.

"It looks absolutely wonderful now. Your little sister has even become a dab hostess in her area!"

"Well, truly, my dear, I am very happy for you, both. I know this isn't a long visit for you-you can't stand to be away from your boys for long. Have supper with us, spend the night, since it will be late, then you can go tomorrow."

"Very well, Russel-one night only. And you're right-I already miss my boys dreadfully!"

And, laughing, brother and sister left the room arm in arm.

55

Ainsleigh Hall (1752)

Lady Madelyn Gaines sat in the Duchess' private parlour. If anyone hadn't seen her in two years, they would not have recognized this attractive woman to be the same, downtrodden duchess of two years past.

Sitting back in her same chair, Madelyn thought about the events of the recent past. She remembered when her son, Peter, then only twelve, came into the room, begging his mother to leave his father. It was that incident, that had gotten Madelyn to realizing that something had definitely to be done. But even so, it was over a year before she had been able to gather enough courage to defy her husband.

She had come up with a plan, but it needed very careful thought. She remembered how she had very thoroughly interviewed various women whose preferences had to be gone into in great detail. She, herself, had been very uncomfortable during these interviews, but they were necessary. Finally, she found the right person.

Annie Hislop was a poor peasant girl whose sexual appetites were almost as bad as those of the Duke-they were, in fact, the perfect pair, thought Madelyn. Furthermore, she was young, clean, and pretty. She will be perfect.

Assigning the girl a suite of simple, plain apartments in the far side of the castle, Madelyn had then gone to her husband.

In no uncertain terms, she had explained to him that she was putting a stop to her treatment by him-before she was killed.

"I am the mother of your child, and do not deserve do be treated in this way. I cannot take it, yet, for you, I have taken it for fourteen years. But it ends now. But I have found someone for you, who will be happy to oblige-her appetites are the same as your's. She is your's-only on the condition you leave me alone."

And the situation had worked out very well. Walter and Annie had latched onto each other beautifully, and Walter no longer terrorized his wife. As for Annie, she was very happy in her new position as mistress of the Duke, and the extra coinage the Duchess slipped her way did her very well, too.

Madelyn rose from her chair, and walked to one of the many mirrors in the room. The face that looked back at her was the face of a woman her age, and a happy woman, at that. Her depraved marriage had stolen years from her, but she had gotten them back. And contentment and peace, she thought-there is nothing more important than that.

And with a little smile, the Duchess of Ainsleigh walked back and sat on her favourite chair, taking up her needlework, while a soft humming escaped her lips.

56

Castle Colbert (1756)

THE Grand Hall of the Castle rang with many voices. The Earl had decided to throw a large party-for the family. And since the family was a large one, it was a large party.

Everyone was dining, and the noise was like Babel.

Russel looked around, and smiled. In his early years, he hadn't really been a family-oriented man. But since the birth of his twins, eleven years ago, he felt he had taken on the role more deeply than would most fathers. This was due to his wife. Russel cast a glance at her, seated next to him. Margarita's profile was, as the rest of her, perfect. She sensed him looking at her, and gave him a smile. The smile contained warmth for him, but it was more the warmth of 'I love you because you're familiar.' Even as she smiled at him, she was looking for a good-looking manservant to bat her eyelashes at. Russel sighed.

As much as he loved her, it had infuriated him that she didn't want anything to do with the raising of their children. It wasn't that she disliked them-she just wasn't interested. So, over the years, Avery and Emma had been delegated to nannies, governesses, tutors, and their father. For them, their mother remained a distant, remote lady of mystery-someone never to be approached.

Smiling, Russel saw his sister, Rhoslyn, and her husband, Timothy. The two of them were perfectly suited. Even now, as they ate, they would say something to each other, then smile, as if they were in their own world. Next, came the Haversleighs, to be exact, mother and son. Roger Haversleigh, now Earl of Stafford, was at twenty-three, a handsome, yet still single, smiling young man. His mother, the Dowager Countess, Camille, was a sweet lady, who liked to talk to people, and was so pleased at seeing the family.

Sitting next to the young Earl was Evelyn Mowbray, aged twenty-two. She was a distant family member of the Mowbray branch. She was an orphan, and was now living at Colbert Castle. Russel caught Roger looking at the young woman from time to time. Grinning inwardly, well, he thought. Perhaps there could be something between them-a wedding next year-or sooner? I know Camille is despairing of Roger ever marrying. And Evelyn is a nice young woman.

Next to Evelyn was fourteen-year-old Alison Treaves-the last living member of the Treaves line. Her entire family had been wiped out by fire, and now she was being raised at Colbert Castle with the others. Just as Evelyn was shy and quiet, Alison was jumpy, and could not sit still. Even now, Russel noticed, she was wolfing her dinner so she could leave and do something more active. She was his daughter's Emma's, best friend. Ah, childhood, he thought.

Russel next turned to look at Madelyn Gaines. She had come with her son-his cousin, Walter, had stayed home with his peasant mistress. Earlier, in his office, Madelyn had told him privately, without mincing her words, exactly the lengths she had gone to, to avoid her husband's ways. To which Russel had said, "You should have done it sooner, my dear. I feel so terrible-I should have done something-and at the very beginning."

"It's no one's fault but mine, for letting it continue. You couldn't have done anything-no one could. But at least it's done now, and Peter and myself can be happy. And, you know, Russel, his way of life is aging him greatly-he looks almost twice his age. I'm sure he isn't a healthy man. As awful as this sounds, I hope God takes him quickly, so that Peter can take over. But at any rate, he is kept occupied, and we are at peace-finally."

Russel hugged his cousin's wife. "Anything you and Peter need, you have only to let me know." Hugging her again, his lips found her's, and the two quickly broke apart. Russel shook his head-no! This was not merely a casual encounter-he sensed it truly meant something.

Looking at the beautiful woman before him, he said, "Who are we trying to fool, Madelyn? What are we trying to deny? We both have unnatural marriages. Why can't we just find some joy in each other?"

After the Duchess' quick nod, Russel then walked to the door of his office, and locked it.

***

Now, after what seemed a hundred years later, Madelyn looked up at the same time, as Russel was watching her. She smiled, and looked down at her plate, continuing to eat, although more animatedly, and with a decidedly becoming blush.

"So *that's* the way it is!" whispered Rhoslyn.

"What is, dear?" Timothy asked. He loved his food, and hadn't looked up from his plate.

"It's Russel! Russel and Madelyn!"

"What about Russel and Madelyn?" Timothy was knawing on his meat, and had barely paid attention to what his wife said.

"Don't you see? Oh my God, that look on her face-she's blissful! Oh, I am so glad! Her husband is a monster, and as for Margarita-well-you know what I call her! If Russel and Madelyn can find happiness with each other, then who is anyone to interfere?"

"Russel and Madelyn? Well, I must say, it's about time."

Rhoslyn turned to look at her husband. Then she kissed his cheek. Tim Albright received the kiss, and continued eating.

57

Castle Colbert (1756)

After dinner, the family met in the large drawing room. The children were there, too. Russel looked first at his two-Avery and Emma. Avery, his heir, the little boy who would inherit all. At the moment, he was yawning heavily after a busy day of play with his cousins. Not so his twin. Emma was still busy playing with her friend and idol-Alison Treaves. Alison, although fourteen, was quite immature for her age, so that eleven-year-old Emma was the perfect playmate. As a result, the two girls got along famously well.

He saw Geoffrey, his nephew. Geoffrey was wide awake, and was trying to persuade cousin Avery for another round of play, to no avail. Russel had to smile, as in frustration, Geoffrey rubbed his bright red hair till it stood up on end.

He was looking at the younger children, when he suddenly noticed eighteen-year-old Peter Gaines playing chess with his cousin, Roger Haversleigh. On looking at Peter, he should have felt some guilt, but he didn't-he was very happy at what he did. True, he had taken it to the full physical level and Margarita didn't, but he had been made to feel a fool throughout his marriage-his wife had played him-and he had let her-he had only himself to blame. No more.

He suddenly realized his feelings for Madelyn went far beyond just lust. His feeling for his wife was lust-but he found he was really beginning to care for the Duchess of Ainsleigh. Can it be, he thought, that I allowed Margarita's behaviour to continue because deep down, I know I didn't really love her? And have I always loved Madelyn-or at least cared for her very deeply? I don't know yet. I don't know if I can call it love-but I do know I care very much for her. That will have to do, for now. The rest may come later.

He suddenly shook his head. What am I thinking? I am married-so is she. I am not thinking divorce for either of us, although Margarita is a tramp, and Walter is a monster. However, that doesn't mean we cannot meet occasionally, and throw off the effects of our marriages. He suddenly smiled. Perfect! I'll work out the details with her in private later. This must continue. Please.

As he was making plans, Margarita herself sat next to him. "Enjoying your party, dear?" She had always found her husband easy to talk with, and she was used to his easy acceptance and few rules. But tonight, she had noticed something different about him. There was a high sense of excitement, happiness, and, yes, virility, that excited her. What was it? Has he found someone? Suddenly, she was jealous. She didn't want Russel with anyone but her; even though she was a flirt, she didn't want her husband to indulge in the same activity. "Shall we retire earlier, my love?" She batted her eyes at him. All of her sensuality was in that question. There were few men around who had been able to resist her when she was working her wiles, as she was tonight. To her surprise, it affected Russel not at all.

"No, I'm going to stay up for a long time. Do not wait for me." Turning to her, he said, "You, Margarita, can do as you please."

58

Castle Colbert (1756)

RUSSEL Carrington-Grey sat at his large desk in the Earl's private office, feeling content. It was the day after the family party, and the family had left-that is, they had all left except Rhoslyn and Timothy. Russel knew he was going to hear from his little sister before she left. She had been exploding to talk to him all through the party weekend, and he had not given her an opportunity.

The Pondshires left first, then the Haversleighs, but not without a betrothal: Roger, the young Earl of Stafford, was betrothed to his distant cousin, Evelyn Mowbray. Both the Dowager Duchess, Camille, and Russel, as Evelyn's guardian, were satisfied as to dowry and settlements. Before leaving, Roger had given his shy bride-to-be a peck on the cheek, causing that young lady to blush furiously, and bow her head. "I'll be seeing you soon!" he called.

Shortly after that, Madelyn had come into his office. He noticed, with rising joy, that she locked the door behind her.

"You've brought ecstasy into my life, Russel, and for that, I thank you. I never knew relations between man and woman could be like this. In my mind, I have always been an innocent-but now, with you, I can't get enough."

She looked pleadingly into his eyes. Knowing what she wanted, Russel walked over to her. "Oh, my love! Yes, I do say love. I think I've loved you for years, but never known it. That door is locked, right?"

Quite some time later, the Duchess of Ainsleigh rose, and said, "Well, I must freshen up. Peter and I must leave soon. Kiss me fervently, here, dearest, as in family company, it must be family kisses." After which, Madelyn left the room, leaving the Earl of Easterbrook in a very happy state indeed.

Now everyone was gone. Even Rhoslyn. But not until she had barged into his office, given him a big hug, and said, "Well done, brother!"

Smiling at his sister's reaction, Russel thought about Margarita. It still didn't bother him. As far as she was concerned, and as far as he felt-the Countess could do as she pleased-he was finally cured of her.

Rising from behind his desk, the Earl walked out of his office, a faraway smile of contentment on his face.

This is the beginning, he thought. After all these years of disappointment and unhappiness for me, and pain for Madelyn, we have both finally been rewarded. It's true what they say: joy comes to those who wait.

Then suddenly, he stopped in his tracks. Oh no. What if a child is the result of this union? It mustn't be. Both he and Madelyn had been so engrossed with their own personal happiness, neither one of them had been thinking of the potential consequences.

Russel sat back down at his desk. Then a slow smile spread across his face. He didn't care. In fact, he would welcome a child of the first and only love relationship he had ever had. Only the future will tell the outcome.

His senses told him-this is only the beginning. It just may be, that by coming together, we have created another branch of the family-he found only pleasure in that thought. I wish I were here a hundred years from now, to see how that branch, and the rest of the family, interacts.

Come what may, the Carrington-Greys will survive. They always have.

～

THE END

I hope you've had as much enjoyment reading
this book, as I have had writing it! NKS

~

～

CPSIA information can be obtained
at www.ICGtesting.com
Printed in the USA
LVOW10s0547240817
546206LV00001B/6/P

9 781525 506383